TARGETED

BECKY AVELLA

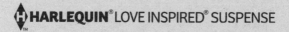

HARLEQUIN® LOVE INSPIRED® SUSPENSE

Recycling programs
for this product may
not exist in your area.

LOVE INSPIRED BOOKS

ISBN-13: 978-0-373-67673-6

Targeted

Copyright © 2015 by Rebecca Avella

www.Harlequin.com

Printed in U.S.A.

A man's heart deviseth his way:
but the Lord directeth his steps.
–Proverbs 16:9

To Pat, my hero and my happily ever after.
We both know this book wouldn't exist without you.

Everyone was in danger because of her.

Stephanie scanned the crowd, assessing the damage. The blast had destroyed their hotel suite and the surrounding rooms. Paramedics worked on a number of people. But it could have been worse.

She turned to Rick. "When we were running, I kept wondering why it took so long for the bomb to detonate." Nothing the serial killer was doing made any sense to her. There had been so many opportunities for him to kill her already. Why did he keep letting her live?

"Maybe the bomb was just a message," Rick replied. "He's telling us that when he is ready to do it, he's going to do it his way."

"By *it*, you mean kill me."

"That's not going to happen, Stephanie." He reached for her hand. "You can't let him get inside your head. Otherwise he accomplished exactly what he set out to do."

He was right, but as she looked across the street, a man standing there pulled her attention. Hadn't the police evacuated the area? Instead of looking at the spectacle around the hotel, he was staring at her. He raised a hand in a wave, and Stephanie's insides turned to ice.

There he was. Her would-be killer.

Becky Avella grew up in Washington State with her nose in a book and her imagination in the clouds. These days she spends her time dreaming up heart-pounding fiction full of romance and faith. Becky married a real-life hero and follows him around begging him to give her material she can use in her stories. Together with their children, they make their home in the beautiful Northwest.

Books by Becky Avella

Love Inspired Suspense

Targeted

ONE

"Seattle Police, K-9 Unit. Announce yourself." Officer Rick Powell's voice boomed through the open door. "If you do not announce yourself, we will send in the dog. If you surrender now, you will not be harmed!"

Rick kept the leash taut and his hand steady on his K-9 partner's back. The dog's training held him still, but Rick knew the Belgian Malinois wanted to go, his muscles quivering to be set free to work again. Only absolute devotion to Rick held the dog back.

Kneeling beside him, Rick crooned the German command for *stay* and stroked the fur along Axle's back. *I understand, buddy. I'm ready to work, too.*

The city block surrounding the early-twentieth-century brick town house had been cordoned off. SWAT team members were poised for action, waiting for the signal that would allow them to penetrate the building, too eager to capture the killer inside to mind the pouring rain running down their stoic faces. Intel indicated the suspect was home and hiding. If their information was correct, then he would soon be calling prison home. Rick believed it was more than he deserved, and it was about time.

"Ready?" Sergeant Terrell Watkins asked Rick.

"Very," Rick answered.

Terrell was Rick's supervisor, but the two had been friends for a long time. It was Rick's first day back on regular duty after an extensive medical leave, and Terrell knew better than any of the others around him how important it was to Rick to be back in the field.

Rick nodded his head in the direction of a wiry man pacing the sidewalk behind the two of them. "But maybe not quite as ready as Shelton is to get this guy."

Terrell's gaze followed where Rick pointed and chuckled. "No kidding."

Detective Gary Shelton deserved the credit for cracking this case. Three unsolved and particularly gruesome murders had terrified the city of Seattle for over a year. It was Shelton who had finally identified Julian Hale as the man responsible for the deaths of those women.

And it was Julian Hale whom they believed was hiding inside this town house now.

Investigating the killings had consumed the detective's life, and bringing Hale to justice had become Shelton's personal mission. They were so close to making that happen. Rick leaned forward, anxious to serve this warrant. He hoped that capturing Hale would allow Shelton some much-earned peace.

Rick called his warning into the house once again, his voice even louder and deeper. "You are surrounded. Announce yourself *now*."

Axle squirmed, his tail thumping on the doorjamb. The dog knew it was go time.

Stroking Axle's fur, Rick's fingers brushed across the healed scar running along the dog's side. Rick had similar scars across his own abdomen. A quick flood of panic raced through his body. Were they both ready to face what was about to go down? *Don't go there. This is a new start, no wallowing in the past.*

"This is your last chance to surrender." Rick's warning echoed into the house, answered only by silence. He unclasped Axle's leash, but kept his hand firm on the dog's back, containing him. Axle's tail thumped harder and faster. No answer came. No one exited the building.

No more chances.

Axle's muscles quivered in anticipation. Rick

might have doubts, but Axle didn't. The dog whined as if to say, "Let me go!"

Pride for Axle pushed away the panic. After a confrontation with human traffickers had left both Axle and Rick near death, the dog had defied all the odds and all of the claims that he would never recover. It was only their first day back, but Rick knew that Axle was stronger than ever and more than capable of doing what was needed. He drew strength from Axle and raised his hand, shouting the command to search. *"Reveire!"*

That one word ignited the built-up energy within Axle's body, propelling the dog forward off his haunches. He disappeared into the house as the men outside waited for barking to alert them to the hidden suspect's location. After several moments of silence, they couldn't wait any longer. The SWAT commander's signal sent Rick and the rest of the Metro team crashing into the house with weapons raised.

The baritone shouts of "Police!" and the urgent calls of "Go, go, go!" harmonized with the high crystal notes of shattering glass, all of it fueling Rick's adrenaline. He caught sight of Axle and trailed after the dog through the chaos, tuning his ears for the sound of barks. *Come on, Axle, show me where the bad guy is hiding.*

Between the men and the dog, the systematic search of the small town house didn't last long. Shout after shout of "Clear!" filled Rick with more disappointment. His sense of justice cried to see this man in handcuffs. Julian Hale had to be in here somewhere.

Rick followed Axle up the stairs to a landing, where he spotted a pull-down attic entrance in the ceiling. He lowered the trapdoor, revealing a wooden staircase. Could Hale be hiding in the attic? Rick trained his gun on the stairs and called out his standard warning one more time. He gave Hale no longer than a heartbeat to comply, then shouted the command to go ahead: "Axle, *geh voraus*!"

Rick envied the dog's unwavering bravery. Without a second of hesitation, Axle shot up the stairs, eager for a new area to search as if he couldn't remember the stabbing they had both lived through. Rick remembered clearly the streetlights flickering off the slashing blade, the sight of Axle airborne, latching his teeth into the man wielding the knife, the feel of pain so searing Rick hadn't been able to believe it was his own. It would all be forever embedded in his memory.

But Axle was right. Those memories had nothing to do with the job at hand. There was a serial killer loose. Getting Julian Hale behind bars before he hurt someone again was the only thing Rick should be thinking about. Axle was relying on his training, and appeared as unwilling to admit defeat as his human coworkers. Taking the dog's lead, Rick shook away the bad memories clouding his mind and focused.

He crouched low, taking the stairs much slower than Axle had done. Although he was convinced by this point that Hale probably wasn't up there, he wasn't taking any chances. He bent and entered the attic space gun first, his eyes fighting to adjust in the dim light coming from a window in the sloped ceiling. The gray drizzle outside made it even darker, but soon his eyes were able to make out the layout of the room.

The attic had been remodeled from its original intended storage space. Two overstuffed chairs and a small love seat were arranged into a conversational sitting space in the center of the room, and a small home office area with bookshelves lined the far wall.

Instead of evoking the cozy feeling it looked as though it should, the room triggered Rick's internal radar. After seven years of law enforcement, he had encountered enough evil to be able to sense when something just wasn't right. Axle's whine confirmed that feeling sending goose bumps popping up along Rick's arm.

Inching his way around the room, Rick

searched every nook or possible hiding place. His jaw clenched. The room was clear. How had Hale gotten away?

He joined Axle by the desk. Rick fumbled with the lamp until he found the switch, illuminating the desk and the wall behind it. Dread settled into his stomach as heavy as if he had swallowed cement.

Two bulletin boards hung on the wall. On the left board there were six photographs stapled in a three-by-two grid. In the second row, Rick recognized the photographs of the three women he already knew Hale had killed. But the upper three photographs were of unfamiliar faces. Were they also victims? Was it possible detectives had missed Hale's connection to other murders? Somehow he knew all of these women were dead. His breathing slowed as he stared at the six pictures. Thinking about the young lives represented in them made the air around him almost too heavy to breathe.

His gaze moved to the second board. White three-by-five cards, small photographs and highlighted spreadsheets were stapled across the outside edges of the board, creating a home-made flowchart, but it was the eight-by-ten photograph in the center that concerned him the most.

Rick studied the girl-next-door beauty smiling back at him from the picture. He noted her heart-shaped face and her long strawberry-blond curls. It was a simple photograph, exactly the type of blue-background portrait that schoolkids brought home each year, or the type that school-teachers had taken for their staff photo. The innocence of it screamed at him. This picture did not belong in the house of a killer.

He spoke into his radio. "Attic's clear, and Sarge?" He swallowed, hating to be the bearer of such bad news, but if anyone could help this woman right now, it was Terrell Watkins. "Sarge, you need to get up here and see this."

His eyes traveled back to the photo. She must be Hale's next victim. Rick groaned. She was out there somewhere in the city, unprotected and unaware that she was standing in the crosshairs of a psychopath.

But that wasn't the worst of it. The worst part was, Rick knew her.

A car in the distance backfired, causing Stephanie O'Brien to drop her keys. She scooped them up and stomped the rest of the way past the playground's graffiti-decorated retaining wall to the front doors of Lincoln Elementary School.

Stephanie rolled her eyes. It wasn't like her to be so jumpy, but about halfway through her trek to the school she had begun to feel as if someone were following her. But every time she peered over her shoulder, she didn't see anyone behind her other than a few bustling people who seemed a lot more concerned with getting out of the freezing rain than with causing her any trouble.

You traveled alone to Africa and back three times before your twenty-fifth birthday, and now you're afraid of walking a few blocks to school? She had hoped that common sense would drive away the uneasiness, but it hadn't. Stephanie pulled her arms in tight to her body and tried to talk herself out of the anxiety creeping up her spine and into her imagination.

To get to the elementary school where she taught fifth grade, Stephanie walked through familiar neighborhoods full of run-down houses that begged for fresh paint and small apartment buildings with rusted metal swing sets in their play areas. Properties and cars were locked behind six-foot-tall chain-link fences, and overgrown, neglected rhododendron bushes commandeered the sidewalk, forcing Stephanie to step into the street if she wanted to pass. Garbage blown out of Dumpsters lay damp along the edges of the buildings and the fences.

The area was a bit rough around the edges, but until today, it had never felt dangerous to her. In fact, these neighborhoods bordered the neighborhood where she lived. Stephanie didn't own a car, so it was routine to trudge back and forth between home and work through this area. It was also common for her to be working in her classroom over the weekend to prepare for the school week ahead. She looked over her shoulder again. This wasn't different from any other trip to school, so why did it *feel* so different?

Tiny droplets from the hood of her raincoat dripped onto her cold nose, reminding her she needed to shake off this silliness and get inside before she drowned. Real Seattleites might be too cool for umbrellas, but at the moment Stephanie would gladly look like a tourist if it meant being dry. It was May for goodness' sake; shouldn't it be warmer?

She glanced over her shoulder one final time before she let herself into the dark building and typed in the security code. The door shut with a *bang* and a *click* as it locked behind her. Other than the squeak of her wet tennis shoes on the waxed tile floor, the hallway stretched into silent darkness.

She flipped on the light in her classroom and locked the door behind her. She threw her keys on her desk and shimmied out of her wet coat. She cranked up her stereo extra loud. The music and the light drove away the eeriness as

Stephanie sat down and grabbed the stack of work waiting for her.

Settling into her chair, Stephanie spread open her lesson plan book and lifted the photo she kept paper-clipped to the inside cover. In the picture she held Moses, the sweet, chubby toddler who had stolen her heart the last time she had visited her younger sister, Emily, in Liberia. Moses's round black face looked straight into the camera, his smile wide, while the photograph captured Stephanie's profile as she stared adoringly at the little boy on her hip. Stephanie's heart lurched with longing as she relived the moment in her mind now.

After her third trip to visit her sister and brother-in-law in West Africa, Stephanie had physically boarded the plane for home, but she had left her heart behind in the red African dirt. Her life now revolved around figuring out how to get back there as a full-time missionary, but the process wasn't going well at all. She didn't have the money to sustain herself without being a burden to Emily and Ty, and with their first baby on the way, they didn't need to take care of her as well on the meager salary they received from an international missions board.

Stephanie swiped her finger across the picture of Moses's face. *I miss you, baby boy. I wonder how big you've gotten this year.* She needed to ask Emily for a more recent picture. She clipped the photo to the book where it belonged, sighed and settled in to do the work in front of her.

An hour passed before the sound of jingling keys in the hallway jerked her attention away from the stack of essays she was reading. The doorknob to her classroom turned. Was a janitor working today? They didn't usually work this late on weekends, but who else would have a master key? Maybe Jim Mendoza, the principal?

Stephanie bit the inside of her cheek. Who was it? Reaching behind her, she fished her cell phone out of the pocket of her wet coat hanging on the back of her desk chair. She glanced at the phone and then tossed it on the stack of papers in front of her. She had forgotten to charge the battery again. Her stomach knotted as she waited for whoever it was behind the door to enter.

"Who's there?" she called.

The door swung open, and a pallid face peeked around it. His washed-out blue eyes widened. "It's just me."

She released all the air she'd been holding as she realized it was the IT guy who had been helping her install all of the new technology she had received from a grant she had won for her classroom. He dropped in unannounced all the time, but this was the first time he had come on a weekend.

Stephanie lowered the stapler in her hand. She must have grabbed it without realizing it before the door opened. Her cheeks burned. She hoped he hadn't noticed the threatening way she had held it. What good would a stapler have done her if it truly had been an emergency?

Her laugh sounded forced and flat in her own ears. "You scared me."

The blond man stood on the classroom door's threshold, his tool bag in hand. He stood perfectly erect, unblinking.

"I didn't mean to startle you," he said. "I didn't expect anyone to be here."

"Did you need anything?"

He pointed at a stack of shipping boxes she hadn't noticed sitting near the front whiteboard. "I thought I would get a head start setting those up for you so you can use them on Monday," he said.

After she won the grant, boxes like these had slowly trickled into her classroom. It felt like Christmas every time a new one arrived. She eyed a large flat box and hoped that the smart board she was looking forward to using was inside it.

Stephanie nibbled on her lower lip, not liking being alone with a man she didn't know well, but she was unsure of what to say or do that wouldn't come across as rude. "Um, sure, I'll just get out of your way, then."

"Thank you, Stephanie."

It was probably nothing more than the over-active imagination she had been combating all day, but something about the way he pronounced her name sent a shiver scampering up her spine. She gathered up her lesson plan book and the stack of essays and moved to the opposite corner from where he stood in the doorway.

"You're welcome, Julian. Let me know if you need anything."

She walked to the round worktable, but before she sat, movement outside startled her.

"Rick?" She cocked her head, confused.

Why was Terrell's friend Rick Powell out there? She gasped. Rick wasn't just standing at the window; his gun was pointing directly at her through the glass.

TWO

Rick's spirits had lifted when he rounded the corner of the school building and saw the glow of artificial light coming from the fourth classroom down the wall. He had hoped he would simply have to knock on Stephanie's classroom window and all of this would be behind them. But once he peeked into her classroom, he knew it wouldn't be that simple.

Even through the window's dirty glass, Rick had recognized Stephanie immediately, but it was the man standing in the doorway behind her, fitting the exact description of Julian Hale, that had caused him to pop back and draw his weapon.

"Freeze!" Rick shouted through the window. He doubted they could hear him clearly, if at all, but he hoped the raised gun made enough of a statement. The glass wouldn't stop him if he had to shoot.

Rick's gaze locked on Hale, trying to anticipate his next move. What was Hale going to do? Run? Try to take out Stephanie? Hale was caught, and Rick expected to read surprise or even fear displayed in the other man's body language. Instead, Hale appeared unfazed by the gun and strangely poised.

Rick needed to get Stephanie out of here and deliver her safely to Terrell Watkins. When they had split up to look for her, Rick had promised Terrell that he would get to her before Hale did. Rick's gut twisted. He had failed to keep that promise.

Terrell and his wife, Val, viewed Stephanie O'Brien as a member of their family. The three of them had known one another for years, and Rick had run into Stephanie so often at their house, he had finally asked Terrell if she was living with them. To which Terrell had laughed and answered, "Practically."

But Terrell wasn't laughing now. Back in the attic, Terrell's broad shoulders had slumped and deep lines of worry had furrowed his forehead as he tried to reach Stephanie on her cell phone.

"My calls are going straight to voice mail," Terrell had said, skimming his tightly cropped black hair with his large hand. "That girl never keeps her cell phone charged, and Val hasn't seen her at all today."

Rick had hated seeing Terrell so upset. The

team counted on their sergeant's lighthearted personality to ease the tense situations. His jokes had gotten Rick through a lot of heavy spots, but with the roles reversed, Rick hadn't known what to say. Finding the photograph of one of your closest friends in the attic of a wanted killer wasn't a light thing.

And now here she was right in front of him. How was he going to get her away from Hale?

Without lowering his gun, Rick reached up and grabbed his mic. "Code 3 assist. I've got a visual on the suspect."

Stephanie wasn't sure which of the two men to look to for answers. She turned back and forth between Rick at the window and Julian in the doorway until it dawned on her. Rick's gun wasn't aimed at her; his target was Julian, and Stephanie was in the way.

She dropped to her stomach, scattering the papers she held in her arms, and scooted toward the window on her belly. Was that the right thing to do? She wished she could read Rick's mind. Right or wrong, she had to put distance between her and the doorway where Julian still stood.

"Stop moving, Stephanie," Julian's icy voice instructed her.

She froze midcrawl. "Why are the police here, Julian? What have you done?"

Although he spoke to her, his eyes stayed on the window and Rick's gun. "I suspect the officer is here not only because of what I've already done, but because he knows what I'm planning to do next."

From her vantage point on the ground, Stephanie looked up and studied Julian's face. A slow, small smile spread, then flickered out, leaving the flat, emotionless affect he always wore. She had noticed his oddities before—his formal speech, erect posture and unwavering calm. She had written them off as nothing more than a social awkwardness from a man who spent all of his time working with computers instead of people. Now she found the same mannerisms cold and calculating.

What are you planning to do?

Fear amplified the flow of blood behind her ears as it raced adrenaline through her body. Her heartbeat paralleled the ticking of the old clock in the front of the classroom. The minute hand kept bouncing into place, marking how long Stephanie lay on the ground waiting for something to happen.

Julian didn't say any more; his eyes remained locked on Rick. She waited for Rick's gun to shatter the glass, but that didn't happen, either.

She remained motionless on her stomach, stuck in the middle of a standoff with no idea what she should do next.

The distant sound of approaching sirens hit her ears. From the sound of it, a lot of law enforcement was about to descend on this place, yet Julian seemed unperturbed by it all. Maybe she could stall him until they arrived.

"What are you planning to do, Julian?" she asked him.

His soulless eyes turned her direction, making her shiver from the coldness she saw in them. "You will have to wait and see, Stephanie. I promise you will know soon enough." Then he bolted from the doorway and disappeared down the dark hallway.

Hammering hit the window above her. Stephanie peered through her lifted arm and watched the old window splinter from the force of Rick's nightstick. Stephanie moved to stand up as Rick raked out the remaining glass, but she fell back down flat again when a large dog flew through the broken window. Stephanie screamed and covered her head.

Rick climbed in the window. "The dog won't hurt you," he reassured her. "Axle, *sitz!*" he commanded, and the dog froze and sat at attention.

"Did you see which way Hale ran?" Rick asked her.

"I don't know. Right, I think?"

Rick spoke into his radio. "Suspect is running toward the front of the school. I won't be able to intercept. Have incoming units set up a perimeter."

Rick squatted beside her. "Are you okay, Stephanie?"

She wanted to yell, *Scared to death, how do you think I'm feeling?* But the concern in his eyes stopped her. "Fine," she told him.

Rick offered Stephanie a hand up, steadying her as she wobbled to her feet. She had been around Rick many times at Val and Terrell's house, but she had never been this close to him. She blushed. The skip in her heartbeat could not be blamed on fear.

"Hale may be hiding in the building. We need to get you to a safer location." Rick let go of her arms and walked to the window. "Can you crawl out with me?"

Stephanie followed him through the window and accepted his outstretched hand on the other side. He guided her to the ground, and the dog leaped through behind them.

"Keep low and stay close behind me. We're going to move along the building to minimize visibility. Understand?"

"Visibility?" she asked him. "Does Julian have a gun?"

Was Julian really that dangerous? She shuddered, thinking of all of the times she had been alone with him in her classroom. What was he capable of doing?

"He's more worried about avoiding capture than he is with hurting you now, but I don't gamble. Stay low."

Rick's long legs covered ground much faster than Stephanie's shorter legs could manage. She jogged behind him trying to keep up. When they rounded the building, Rick called to her over his shoulder, "The cavalry has arrived."

Patrol car after patrol car surrounded them, filling the parking lot. The flashing lights and number of arriving vehicles mesmerized her. People in a variety of uniforms and suits piled out of their cars, sprinting in different directions.

All of this for Julian? A typical criminal would not invite this intense of a response, would he? She spotted uniforms from Seattle Police Department and King County Sheriff's Office and read "SWAT" on the back of several officers advancing on the building. She swallowed as her eyes landed on the FBI label on the side of a parked SUV.

Rick placed a warm hand on the small of Stephanie's back and guided her to the passenger door of a blue patrol car with "K-9" painted on the side.

"Watch your head," he said.

She backed down onto the passenger seat facing out. Rick kept his hand on the door and knelt in front of her. His nearness and direct gaze made her squirm. "Did Hale hurt you at all?"

She blushed and shook her head. "No. Julian had just arrived. He hadn't even stepped out of the doorway before you came."

"Did he say anything to you?" Rick eyes roved across her face, looking as if he thought he would be able to read what he wanted to know written there. But she didn't have any answers. She didn't know what he needed her to tell him.

"I don't know. He said that you knew what he was planning to do next, or that you knew what he had already done, or something like that." She closed her eyes trying to remember more, anything that would be useful.

"Did he say where he was going? What his plans were specifically?"

"No. I told you, Rick. I don't know anything. He wasn't making any sense. When I asked him what he was talking about, all he said was that I would know soon enough, and then he ran down the hall."

"That's it? You're sure you can't remember anything else? This is important, Stephanie."

It felt as though he was interrogating her. "I told you everything I can remember. There wasn't time for anything else." She looked down into Rick's upturned face. His expression was hard, his mouth a straight line. She knew he wanted her to give him some clue, but she wanted some answers of her own. "Rick, you need to tell me what is going on."

He stood up and leaned in close so she could hear his words above the racket. "I need to talk to these guys and then we'll get out of here, okay?"

"Okay," she said, turning forward so her feet were in the car. Then the door slammed shut, leaving her alone in the silence to try to sort through all of the activity happening around her. He hadn't answered her question.

She scanned the bustling crowd outside the car and found Rick's tall form. He stood side by side with two other Seattle PD officers, each with their arms crossed over their chest, deep in serious conversation. Set in this scene, Rick's natural presence and rugged good looks made it easy to pretend he was the star of some crime show on prime time. But this was real life, and somehow she was involved in it. How had her quiet afternoon of lesson planning morphed into a TV drama?

Rick's dog waited at his side. His alert ears and long black snout reminded Stephanie of a German shepherd, but his coloring was a light brown and he seemed too small for a shepherd. Whatever breed he was, Stephanie could read the mutual devotion dog and handler had for each other. This dog didn't fit the image she had of intimidating and snarling K-9 dogs. This one looked more like an overgrown puppy with his tail in constant wag mode.

For the briefest moment, Rick's gaze held hers through the windshield. Her stomach tightened, and she held her breath. Time stretched, feeling longer than four heartbeats. What was he thinking? Had they caught Julian?

Rick's eyes remained fixed on where she sat watching him inside the car. He finished his conversation and walked away from the other officers, his dog jogging along beside him. *Finally, he'll be able to tell me what is going on.*

Rick opened the rear door, allowing the dog to jump into the kennel in the back of the car. "Stephanie, meet Axle. Axle, meet Stephanie."

Stephanie smiled over her shoulder. "Hey, Axle. Nice to meet you."

Rick climbed into the front seat next to her. Stephanie turned her smile to him. "I'm not sure what all of this is about, but somehow I think I need to thank you for coming to my rescue."

"My pleasure, Miss O'Brien," he said in a bad impression of John Wayne. Rick's smile was wide and genuine, revealing a dimple in his left cheek she hadn't noticed before.

"Did you catch Julian?" *Are you going to tell me who he really is? What you want him for?*

Rick's smile faded. "No, he got away from us for the second time today." He maneuvered the car out of the parking lot. "Our job's not done yet. He's still loose, and he's still a threat."

A stab of guilt hit Stephanie. Maybe Rick could have caught Julian if he hadn't stopped to take care of her first. "I'm sorry I kept you from going after him."

"No. Don't be sorry." He averted his eyes and quietly added, "You have no idea how happy I was to find you safe, and not..."

Stephanie waited for him to fill in that blank, but he let it drop. "Not what?" she probed.

Instead of a direct answer, he started the car's ignition and said, "I'm under strict orders to deliver you to Terrell. He'll fill you in on everything when we get to his house."

Then he winked at her, and his dimple made its second appearance. "Right after he finishes yelling at you for not charging your cell phone."

THREE

Rick maneuvered around the tricycle blocking the walkway leading up to the Watkinses' modest blue bungalow. He gestured for Stephanie to climb the steps to the front door ahead of him. Savory aromas wafted out to them like a welcoming committee. Rick's stomach contracted, begging him to feed it. It had been a long day with no food, and his shift didn't end for another two hours, and that was only if he didn't get held for overtime. Rick couldn't help but hope Val would feed him before he rejoined the search for Hale. Nothing he could make for himself or grab at a drive-through window would compare to her cooking.

Valencia Watkins came from a long line of Latina women famous for their skill in the kitchen. She did not believe a single bachelor could cook well enough to keep himself alive. All six feet five inches of her well-fed African-American husband revealed how Val loved people. She fed them, and one bite of her cooking had forever convinced Rick he would never turn down an offer to eat at her table.

"Mmm. I can smell Val's cooking all the way out here," Stephanie said. She gave him a crooked half smile. The urge to do or say something to make that smile reach her eyes, to light up her face as it usually did, hit him hard.

It relieved Rick to deliver Stephanie here. With Hale loose, she wasn't completely safe, but he couldn't imagine her being in much danger in this place. This little blue house full of good smells and toys underfoot always felt like a haven to him.

The Watkinses' six-year-old son, Joash, answered the doorbell. His dark eyes lit up when he saw Rick and Stephanie standing on his front porch. The boy hugged Stephanie, then he turned to Rick and lifted the baseball mitt on his left hand. "It isn't raining as hard now. Wanna come out and play catch with me?"

"Sorry, Joe. Can't today, I'm working." As he ruffled the boy's black hair, the gesture left him hollow. Although he often ruffled the fur on top of Axle's head, this time the motion reminded him of someone else.

Allie.

Rick hadn't allowed himself a conscious thought about his former fiancée in a long time.

It was always safer to block memories after she called off their engagement, but every once in a while a stray one like this floated to the surface before he could stop it.

Allie had always been so proud of her glossy dark hair. She would spend hours fixing it with a pile of products and styling tools Rick couldn't imagine counting. Sometimes he would be a pest and mess up her hair on purpose, but other times it was simply an unconscious show of affection. Regardless of what his intentions might have been, Allie's response had always been the same: ducking, slapping away his hand and moaning, "Knock it off, Rick, I just fixed my hair." He figured the rich, ambulance-chasing attorney that Allie had married this past summer never messed up her hair like that. Rick shoved his memories down deep where they belonged and commanded them to stay put, turning his attention back to his friends in the present.

Terrell stood in the doorway and waved them inside while Joash ran through the house announcing their arrival, "Mama! Stephanie and Officer Powell are here!"

Val appeared with her three-year-old daughter, Hadassah, trailing behind her. When Val saw Stephanie, she said, "Stephanie. Thank God you are all right."

"Hi, Haddie," Rick said to the little girl. She hid behind her mom, but peeked out around her to grin at him.

Val wrapped Stephanie up into her arms. "I have been so worried about you."

"Thanks, Val," Stephanie told her friend. She glanced from Val to Rick to Terrell. "I'm fine. Still a little confused about what's going on, though."

Rick winced. He should have told her something during the car ride from the school to the Watkinses' house. Even if it were glossed over, some information would have helped to put her mind at ease, but no matter how he rehearsed it in his head, the explanation kept sounding something a little like, *Hey, Stephanie, you know that serial killer the news has been talking about for the past year. Guess what? That's Julian Hale. And by the way, I sure like your last staff photo. Hale must have liked it, too, because he has it pinned to his "People to Kill Next" bulletin board.*

He had never been known for his eloquence, especially with women. Eventually she had stopped asking, making the rest of the car ride quiet and awkward. He had convinced himself that not answering her was the right thing to do. Terrell and Stephanie had a long history together. He would know best how to tell her.

They all stepped into the living room. Terrell's raised eyebrows asked Rick behind Stephanie's back, *you didn't tell her?*

Rick shook his head negative.

"Come eat," Val said. "You, too, Rick," she instructed. "Everything will seem better on a full stomach."

Rick's grinned, "Well, if you *insist*."

"I insist," Val informed him as she ushered Stephanie out of the living room and into the kitchen to help her put the meal on.

"You didn't tell her anything about Hale yet?" Terrell asked him as soon as Stephanie was out of earshot. When Rick shrugged his shoulders, Terrell rolled his eyes and shook his head, "Didn't know you were a coward, Powell."

"Ha!" Rick pointed a finger at Terrell. "You just wish I had gotten it over with so you wouldn't have to break it to her yourself."

"Guilty as charged. Hopefully Val is telling her now." Terrell clapped a large hand on Rick's shoulder. "Well, you heard the lady. Check out for your lunch break, and let's get in there and eat." Then he added, his signature goofy grin back in place, "Like I always say, don't try to catch a serial killer on an empty stomach."

"That's what you always say, huh?" Rick chuckled and then checked out on his radio. He would have thirty minutes to eat before he had to get back to work. He hoped an urgent call wouldn't come over the radio before he got to taste what he could smell. Lunch break or not, he had to run when certain calls came over the air, even if it meant leaving Val's amazing cooking behind.

Joash ran into the room and tugged on his arm. "Can I say hi to Axle?"

"If there's time, I'll get him out for a bit after we eat, but Axle and I and your dad have some important work to do today."

Joash beamed and smacked an imaginary ball into the baseball mitt he still wore. "Officer Powell, can I sit next to you at dinner?"

"Sure, bud." Joash was such a cute kid, with his missing front teeth. Rick had tried to get Joash and Haddie to call him by his first name long ago, but Terrell had put the kibosh on it, insisting the kids remain respectful and use his title. Rick wondered how Stephanie had managed to get them to call her by her first name.

Haddie reached her little arms up to her dad. Terrell swung her up to his shoulder one-handed. Haddie squealed, delighted.

The domestic bliss of this house hit Rick the way it always did: with envy. It was the future he had dreamed of having with Allie, although now that he had moved past the initial pain of their breakup, he could admit there was nothing about this scene that Allie would have wanted. While he had been dreaming of backyard barbecues, T-ball games and ballet recitals, Allie had been dreaming of foreign cars, exotic vacations and a sprawling home in Medina where she could host cocktail parties.

But even if she had wanted this kind of life, the scars on Rick's stomach reminded him of the danger and demands of his job. Could he blame Allie for walking away? Some guys learned how to be a cop and maintain relationships, but the statistics proved that not many did it well. Terrell Watkins had it figured out, it seemed, but Rick didn't know the secret.

"Duck your head, baby girl," Terrell said before he led them through the arched doorway.

Entering the kitchen, Rick's eyes found Stephanie's pale face. Her lips were tight, as if she were afraid to breathe. He looked at her hand gripping the countertop, and he knew that she knew.

Val had wanted to eat before talking, but Stephanie wouldn't have it. There was no way she was going to sit patiently through a meal pretending that there wasn't a weighted secret hovering above everyone's heads. As soon as they were alone in the kitchen, she'd grabbed Val's arm and demanded to be told the truth.

"All three of you know something you aren't telling me," she had insisted. "I'm a big girl, Val. What is going on?"

So Val had held her hand and told her everything she knew about Julian Hale. Now Stephanie wished she could take it back. Maybe she wasn't such a big girl, after all, because she didn't want *this* truth. Stephanie held on to the edge of the counter to steady herself. The solid surface squeezed between her fingers and thumb gave her something real to grasp when everything around her felt dreamlike. *Julian Hale is a murderer. I've been alone with him many times. He has killed before, and he wants to kill me.*

Another question nagged at her subconscious, begging to be answered. *Why hasn't he tried to kill me already? He's had so many opportunities.* Somehow she knew that today had been the day he planned to do it.

Her gut ached as she watched Terrell lifting Haddie off his shoulders. Yes, she wanted to return to Africa and to mission work, but she also dreamed of being married someday. She dreamed of having a family of her own like this one, with kids like Haddie and Joash, and a husband who loved her the way that Terrell loved Val. If Rick Powell hadn't shown up exactly when he had, Julian could have killed her today. He could have blotted out her future completely.

Then she remembered the worst of it. *He is still out there. They haven't caught him yet.* Fear swam through her, blurring her vision.

Val ushered the two kids to the sink to wash their hands for dinner. Stephanie glanced at them, making sure they were out of earshot. "Thank you, Rick," she squeaked out. "Thank you for finding me in time." The words were inadequate, but she didn't know what else to say.

Rick sucked his lips inward and breathed through his nose deeply. His hand curled as if he were fighting the urge to punch something. "You're welcome, Stephanie. I wish we had caught him so you wouldn't have to be afraid."

As their eyes met, Stephanie tried to send her gratitude across the space between them. An unexpected urge to walk right into his arms overcame her. She longed to be held by someone stronger than she was, to have muscular arms wrap around her, making her feel safe again. It was a silly thought, though, and if she acted on it she would look like a fool. Rick was nothing more than an acquaintance. After he ate this meal, he would leave. He would return to his own life and his own problems.

Her throat thickened as loneliness joined her fear. She needed family to turn to, but she didn't have anyone close enough to help her. She had Val and Terrell, but they had a real family of their own to worry about. Her sister was in Africa, and the last time Stephanie had spoken to her immature and unreliable mother, she was living in Eastern Oregon working at some casino. Stephanie sneered at the thought of calling her. Somehow her mother would find a way to spin Stephanie's problems into being all about her, anyway. And her father wasn't an option, either. He had walked out on their family when Stephanie was the same age as Haddie. She couldn't even remember what he looked like. There was nobody. There never had been.

Stephanie had always taken care of herself and everyone else, as well. Her mom had fallen apart after her dad deserted them, leaving Stephanie to raise her little sister. Stephanie had paid her own way through school and Emily's Bible college bills, too. She had never expected anyone to take care of her, but nothing she had faced up to this point had felt so big and so completely beyond her own ability to handle.

All of her energy was gone, her arms suddenly too heavy to lift. "I don't know what to do," Stephanie admitted. Tears pooled, threatening to fall.

Val's arm circled her waist. "We'll figure it

out together, honey." She guided Stephanie into a chair at the table. "And in the meantime, we eat."

Chairs scraped across the hardwood floor as everyone took a seat, crowding around the small round oak table. Val and Terrell nestled close together, and Haddie and Joash sat beside each of them. Rick scooted his squeaky chair in next to Stephanie, so close she could feel the heat radiating from his leg. The realization of his nearness made heat move through her own body to her cheeks.

She couldn't count how many times she had been in this house feeling like a third or fifth wheel. That is, unless someone had been playing matchmaker, then of course she would be sitting next to some awkward blind date. But this felt different, comfortable even. If the reason they were here together wasn't so heavy, she would choose to stay in this moment for a long time.

You are grasping for security, Stephanie O'Brien. You are scared, and Rick saved you today. That's all this is. Don't read any more into it than that.

Stephanie wiggled in her chair. Thank goodness no one could read her mind and see her silly fantasy. Rick Powell wasn't even her type. He couldn't be. He had a career in Seattle and a purpose to fulfill here. She wasn't his type, either. If she could stay alive long enough to do it, she was moving to Liberia full-time. Stephanie wanted a life like the one her sister had found when she married Ty and started their mission work together. The right man for her would want that, too.

She caught Rick's profile in her peripheral vision. His espresso-colored hair was cropped short on the sides, but he kept it a bit longer and messier on top. She liked how his strong square jaw saved him from looking too cute. She had never been a fan of men who looked like catalog models. The skin around his hazel eyes crinkled kindly as he smiled at a story Joash was telling him.

Stephanie sighed. As good as it felt to forget about Julian Hale for a minute and pretend she was here with this attractive man in a uniform, it could never be more than a fun diversion. They were two people on different life tracks.

"Hadassah Grace, it's your turn to say the blessing," Terrell told his daughter.

Haddie stuck her fingers in her mouth and shook her head with vigor. "Huh-uh. You pray, Daddy." She hid her face in her mom's arm. Stephanie had never seen the spunky girl so bashful. Rick Powell's presence must be affecting both of them. *No one can blame us, Haddie. He is cute.*

Terrell grasped Val's hand on his right and Joash's hand on his left. Stephanie jumped as Rick's large hand wrapped around her smaller one. She had forgotten about the Watkins family tradition of holding hands when they prayed. Stephanie relaxed and wrapped her fingers around Rick's palm, feeling his calluses and his strength. Tears pricked her eyes again as Haddie's little fingers grasped her other hand. Stephanie was so grateful to be a part of this circle.

"Father, we thank You for the blessing of this food," Terrell prayed. "We praise You that Stephanie is safe with us, and we pray that You would continue to watch over her and protect her. Grant her peace and the ability to trust You. Equip Rick and me in our work and help us to bring Julian Hale to justice soon."

Amens circled the table, but Rick did not drop Stephanie's hand after the last one. Instead, he squeezed it. She met his gaze. His eyes were amazing. If she had to define the color, she would probably call them hazel, but they had a metallic, reflective quality that gave them a silvery glow. She forgot to blink.

"We'll find him, Stephanie. I won't stop until we do."

"Thank you, Rick," she whispered. Once

again she hoped he knew how much that meant to her.

During the rest of the dinner they all tried valiantly to keep the tone light. The kids finished earlier than the adults and were excused to watch a cartoon and eat their dessert in the living room. Joash skated around the kitchen in his socks, while Haddie bobbed with excitement. Val didn't let them eat outside the kitchen often.

Stephanie had hardly tasted her food. It was difficult to swallow anything with her stomach in so many anxious knots. She tried to decline dessert, but Val set the pie and mug of hot coffee in front of her despite her protests.

"You are an evil temptress," Stephanie accused her. Val returned a smug smile.

"Hey, you can tempt me all you want," Terrell informed his wife, patting the empty spot at the table in front of him. "Where's my pie?"

"I'll eat yours for you, Stephanie," Rick teased. He leaned back in his chair and winked. "It's a dirty job, but…" He shrugged.

Stephanie pulled her pie close and encircled it with her arms. "Back off, Powell. Now that it's in front of me, it's all mine."

The laughter swirled around her, lifting the weight off her chest. *Could we all just stay right here, happy and safe like this?* But she knew they couldn't. It was too soon before Terrell and

Rick pushed back from the table, their half-hour lunch break long past.

Terrell pulled Val into his arms and kissed her forehead. A pang of jealousy hit Stephanie as it always did when the Watkinses were affectionate in front of her. Terrell and Val fit together; they had always been a perfect match. What would it feel like to be loved like that?

Terrell walked to Stephanie's chair and squeezed her shoulder. "Until Hale is captured, I think it is a good idea for you to stay here with us," he told her. "I can drive you over to your place after work to pick up whatever you need."

"I don't want to put you guys in danger," Stephanie protested. "You said Julian has been following me and had a detailed list of all of my activities. I'm sure your address showed up on that chart a few times."

"It's a risk we are willing to take," Val said, her hands on her hips. "You can't go back to your house alone."

Stephanie didn't like the idea, but where else could she go? Should she try to leave town? What about teaching in the morning? Should she show up at her school or take a leave of absence?

Question after question marched across her mind demanding answers, making her head pound. There were so many details to figure out. She would impose on Terrell and Val only as long as it took for her to figure out an alternative plan.

Haddie waddled into the kitchen rubbing her eyes. Stephanie didn't know a more adorable little girl. Haddie's creamy brown skin and melted-chocolate eyes came from Val, but the black hair that her parents left all natural came from her daddy. She always wore bows or headbands, but her beautiful hair made a statement all by itself. Haddie was a walking, talking reminder of Stephanie's dreams for the future. She reminded Stephanie of all of the girls waiting for her in the Liberian orphanages. Stephanie wanted to fill up those hungry little girls until they radiated as much life, love and health as this sweet girl did.

"Mommy," Haddie said to Val. She crinkled her button nose. "I no like smoke."

Val scooped her into her lap. "What, baby? Are you sleepy?"

"No, I not sleepy!" Haddie pounded her fists on her thighs. She tried to get her point across again, "I said, I no like..." but if she finished the sentence, it was impossible to hear her tiny voice over the screaming smoke detector.

FOUR

The demanding wails of the fire alarm assaulted Rick's ears as fingers of smoke slithered into the kitchen along the ceiling. The acrid scent and quickly filling air left no doubt that they were dealing with real fire. One of the chairs crashed backward, but no one bothered to set it back up in their haste to escape.

Haddie plugged her ears, her wails competing in volume with the alarm. "Turn it off, Daddy. Turn it off!"

Rick yelled for help into his radio, hoping dispatch could make sense of his words on their end because he was struggling to hear their responses back to him.

"Go to the alley!" Terrell shouted as he pushed the women and Haddie out the kitchen door into the backyard.

The encroaching smoke drove Rick and Terrell to their knees in search of fresher air. Rick began crawling on all fours toward the living room, but Terrell grabbed his shoulder and hollered, "I'll get Joash," Terrell pointed at the back door. "The girls shouldn't be out there alone."

Did Hale do this? Rick crawled fast for the back door, wondering if the women were in more danger outside all alone than if they had stayed together. Emerging from the house, he drank in the rain-washed air in greedy gulps, thankful to be free of the choking smoke. His eyes still burned as he ran toward the women and Haddie. Although they looked unharmed, their faces were slack with shock, and the orange glow flickering in their eyes made Rick dread turning around to look for himself.

The little blue house, the sweet haven Rick loved, was reducing to a glowing skeleton before his eyes. Giant tongues of fire licked the roofline, then converged into pillars of flame and black smoke billowing into the late-afternoon sky. Burning bits and pieces of the house floated on the air before landing on wet grass and smoldering out. The fire had already consumed the front half of the house, and the glow from the back windows said the kitchen would be next.

Rick imagined the family photos hanging on the walls. He pictured the kids' bedrooms and their toys. He saw all of the little things that made Val and Terrell's house a home. He couldn't stand the thought of it all burning. This was not right, and if this was Hale's doing, he would pay for it. Rick would make sure of it.

Rick leaned toward the house, eager to go back for Terrell, but the women beside him needed him, too. He was torn about who needed him the most. *Hurry up, Terrell. Get out of there.*

The insistent syllables of approaching sirens confirmed the chattering radio in his ear. Responders were almost there. Rick placed a hand on Val's shoulder and tried to comfort her, "Can you hear that, Val? They're on their way to help. It's going to be okay."

Both Stephanie and Val turned worried eyes to him. Val shifted Haddie to her opposite hip and asked, "But where are Terrell and JoJo? Why aren't they out here yet?"

"They're coming," Rick assured them, hoping he spoke the truth. Stephanie gave him a look behind Val's back. Her expression and raised eyebrow seemed to silently ask him, *are they?*

Stephanie took Haddie from Val's arms. "Sweetie," she asked the girl, "where was Joash in the house?"

"Him's sleeping," Haddie answered and pointed to the house. "On the couch in the libbing room."

Rick tensed. It was only late afternoon. Being

asleep this early in the day did not seem right for the active little boy. Had Joash already succumbed to smoke inhalation? His eyes scanned the house, searching for signs of Terrell and his son. Would he need to go in after them?

Another flame leaped high into the sky, directly above where Haddie last saw Joash. Still Terrell did not appear, but they couldn't wait in the alleyway any longer. If it was Hale who had set the fire, he could still be nearby, and if he was, the isolated alleyway wasn't the best place to protect everyone. Setting a fire in broad daylight showed just how bold Hale was willing to be. They had to move even if it meant temporarily abandoning Terrell and Joash.

"We need to get out front," he told the women. Hopefully the growing crowd of emergency vehicles and curious neighbors would spook Hale enough to keep him far away for the time being. Rick was also concerned about Axle. Rick couldn't imagine how freaked out the dog must be stuck inside the backseat kennel with all this commotion going on around him.

He ran a few paces down the alley before realizing that Val and Stephanie weren't following him. "Come on." But Val stood her ground. She seemed unable to turn from the burning inferno that held her husband and her son.

Stephanie balanced Haddie on her hip, then

grabbed Val's hand and tugged. "Come on, Val. Maybe Terrell and Joash went out the front door. We need to follow Rick."

Finally, Val relented. They all jogged down the alley to a place where they could safely cut through a neighbor's backyard, stepping onto the front sidewalk at the same moment that the first of the fire engines arrived. An ambulance parked behind the engine, and then behind that, Terrell ran from the same neighbor's yard with Joash in his arms. Rick's shoulders slumped in relief.

"*¡Gracias a Dios!*" Val cried out, thanking God out loud with every step as she ran to her husband and son. Haddie wiggled out of Stephanie's arms and joined her family, leaving Rick and Stephanie alone by his patrol car, where they could hear the muffled sounds of Axle's anxious barks coming through the windows.

Rick opened the kennel in the back, and an agitated Axle flew out onto the sidewalk, running circles around Rick's legs, unsure of which direction he wanted to go. Rick squatted and pulled Axle in close. He massaged big fistfuls of fur along Axle's neck, trying to calm the dog with his voice and touch. "You're okay, buddy. Everything's okay." It took extra effort, but once Axle was reassured, Rick was able to turn his focus back to Stephanie. She stared at the burning house, hardly blinking. Creases formed between her eyes. He stood back up, not liking the look on her face.

"Are you okay, Stephanie?"

She didn't answer him, just hugged her bare arms around her slim waist and shivered. He grabbed a blanket from the trunk and wrapped it around her shoulders. "Didn't your mama ever tell you not to go out in the rain without a coat?"

She humored him with a small smile and a quick, absentminded "thanks" for the blanket and returned her attention to the fire.

Given the circumstances, it wasn't the most relevant or professional thing to be focusing on, but Rick couldn't help noticing how pretty Stephanie looked. Even after all that she had endured today—crawling through windows, running away from a psychopath, escaping a burning building—Stephanie was still stunning.

It wasn't the first time Rick had noticed her beauty. He had always thought of her as an attractive girl, but watching her now he was struck by how naturally that beauty came to her. It was effortless. Without a bit of makeup, standing in drizzling rain, she was beautiful. He thought of the photo of her hanging on Hale's attic wall. He saw again the joy in her eyes and her easy smile. He did not like seeing anxiety dimming that joy.

Without turning her head from the scene in front of her, Stephanie said to him, "This is because of me, isn't it." She didn't say it like a question. She was declaring what she had already decided to be true.

He turned her by the shoulders to face him before he said, "This is not your fault, Stephanie. That is an old house with outdated wiring, and a chimney that probably hasn't been cleaned in a while. It could have been any number of things that started that fire." She tried to turn away, but he held her shoulders and made her look him in the eyes. "I mean it. This is not your fault."

"But look what I've brought on my friends," she said, gesturing toward the house. "They do not deserve this." The anxiety he had seen on her face hardened into determination. Stephanie looked him in the eyes and said, "I know they will still want me to stay with them. But I can't. I will not put them in any more danger. Wherever I go, I know that Julian will follow."

Rick looked down into her determined face, respecting the strength of character he saw there. But he also felt her fine-boned shoulders under his hands, and an urge to protect her surprised him. Years of training and experience told him not to get involved. He had to do whatever he could to keep his professional distance. If he let things get personal, the job would consume him.

Yet here he was, holding a pretty girl by the shoulders, searching her anxious eyes for something he could do or say that would do any good, discovering that as foolish as it may be, he did not want to keep his distance.

He wanted to give her more than a pep talk, but it was all he had at the moment. "Look, you've been through a terrible day. Don't worry about anything until we know more. One thing at a time, okay?"

He left one hand on her shoulder and looked toward the ambulance. Joash wore an oxygen mask and was being loaded into the back of the truck. Terrell sat on the back edge with his own oxygen mask while Val and Haddie climbed inside with Joash.

Watching them, Rick remembered the long hours Terrell had sat by him in the hospital when he was recovering from the stabbing. He remembered how Val had stocked his freezer with ready-to-eat meals, and how they had cared for Axle until Rick was on his feet again. The Watkinses were the best kind of people, the best kind of friends. Now they were facing their own crisis. It was his turn to step up and help them.

And he suddenly knew the best thing he could do to help.

"Stay right here," he told Stephanie. "I need to talk with Terrell."

Julian Hale.

Until this afternoon, Stephanie hadn't known Julian's last name. In her mind, he had simply been Julian, the IT guy. She had never talked to him much, because he seemed like the kind of guy who was happiest when you got out of his way and left him alone to work. Any small talk she had attempted only seemed to make him uncomfortable, so whenever he was in her classroom, she would leave. She would walk down the hallway to the office to make copies or check her always-overflowing mailbox, anything she could find to burn the time. On the days she had chosen to stay in her classroom, she had purposefully kept the chitchat to a minimum for his sake. She had thought that was what he wanted her to do.

For as little as she knew of him, he apparently knew all about her, though. Every. Detail. Rick and Terrell had told her about the bulletin board in his attic. She shivered at the thought of her school picture stapled up there. Julian probably knew her middle name and her social security number. What other trivial details of her life had he uncovered? Did he know the name of her kindergarten teacher? Or what kind of cereal she liked to eat in the morning?

Stephanie pulled the blanket Rick had given her tighter around her shoulders. What she really wanted to ask was *why me?* What was it about her that had convinced Julian she deserved to die? She thought she had been kind to him. What had made him hate her so much that he wanted to kill her?

Another patrol car pulled in behind the ambulance where Rick stood talking with Terrell. Terrell had slipped off his own oxygen mask, and the two men kept glancing her way. Stephanie cringed. *They are trying to figure out what to do with me.*

She hated being a burden. She preferred the caretaker role. It had always been important to her to be strong and independent, not needy and self-centered like her broken mother. This whole situation had slipped out of her control. Somehow she needed to take it back, to take care of herself instead of standing here waiting for Val and Terrell to make everything better for her, or for Rick Powell to feel he had some kind of obligation to become her knight in shining armor.

It looked as though the firefighters were gaining the advantage over the fire. Would the house ever be what it once was? She closed her eyes. *Thank you, Lord, that everyone got out okay.*

She knew this was her fault. She might not have lit the match, but she did not believe this was an accident. How else would her friends suffer if they continued trying to protect her? What would Julian try next time that could hurt them? Stephanie slipped the blanket off her shoulders, folded it and placed it on the hood of Rick's car. She wasn't going to let there be a next time.

By the ambulance, Rick nodded at something Terrell said, and then he turned his body with his back toward her blocking Terrell from her view. Rick leaned in closer, absorbed in their conversation. This was her cue to exit. She could slip away now while Val was preoccupied with the kids and paramedics and Terrell was talking to Rick. She had to do this her own way, but Val and Terrell would stop her if they knew what she planned to do.

Stephanie stopped a passing paramedic. He didn't look too busy, or in too much of a hurry to get somewhere else, but it still embarrassed her to interrupt him from his work. She couldn't just disappear, though. Taking off with no explanation would send them all looking for her again. "Excuse me," she asked him, her voice too squeaky. She cleared her throat and tried again. "Do you happen to have a piece of paper and a pen I could borrow?"

"Yeah, sure." He pulled a small notepad and pen from the breast pocket on his uniform. Ripping off a sheet of paper, he handed both to her. "Just keep the pen."

The paramedic walked a few paces away, then turned. "Hey, weren't you inside the house? Has anyone checked you out yet?"

Stephanie hated lying to him, but she hadn't been near the fire long enough to inhale any smoke. The longer she stood around chatting, the more her window for slipping away undetected was shrinking.

"Yeah. I'm good. Thanks for the pen." She flashed him what she hoped was a confident "I'm just fine" smile. He nodded and left her to fend for herself.

Using Rick's patrol car hood as a hard surface, Stephanie wrote a quick message:

T and Val—I know you want to help me, but you have enough to deal with right now. Don't worry about me.

I promise I'll be smart. Praying for you guys. I'll check in soon. Love, Stephanie.

And Rick—Thanks again for all your help. I'm pretty sure you literally saved my life today. I'm grateful.

She anchored the paper with Rick's windshield wiper. When she turned, she saw Axle standing on the sidewalk watching her. He cocked his head, looking curious.

"Take care of them for me, okay, Axle?" The dog wagged his tail.

She didn't have a plan yet, not even a clue where she should go first. She did know, however, that she could not stick around and allow Julian Hale to harm little Haddie or Joash or their parents any more than he already had done.

It was cold, and it was wet. She had no coat, no money and no cell phone. She had no idea what came next, but Stephanie put one foot in front of the other, determined to lead Julian Hale away from the people she loved.

FIVE

"Are you sure?" Terrell sat on the back edge of the ambulance. His eyes blinked rapidly as he gaped at Rick. "I mean, I'm thankful for your help, but you've worked so hard to get back out in the field. It's been such a long road to recovery. I would never dream of asking you to put that on hold, especially not on your first day back on duty."

Rick kicked a pebble away with the toe of his boot. He rammed his hands deep into his pockets and fiddled with a challenge coin he always carried. Was he sure? The decision was made—he was going to protect Stephanie and help Terrell and Val. It wasn't about what he did or did not *want* to do. This was about the meaning of friendship.

He swallowed down what he wanted. He wanted to be a member of his team again and to be back at work with Axle. Law enforcement was his calling. It ran in his blood. His grandfather, his dad and his uncle were all retired cops. Rick had not been one of those kids who followed in his family's footsteps because he thought it was what he was supposed to do. Rick had become a cop because it was what he loved to do. The whole first year of work at SPD, he had marveled at the thought, *I'm getting paid to do this?* Eventually over the years, he had settled into it being demanding work with a lot of sacrifice involved. His failed relationship was proof of that, but through it all there had been a sense that he was doing what he was meant to do. Being injured for so long and cut off from that world had made him feel lost.

Rick cleared his throat. If he thought about this for too long, he might wimp out and take back his offer. "Getting back to work can wait," he told Terrell. "It shouldn't take you that long to get your family squared away. Besides, after all that you and Val did for me and Axle, it's the least I can do."

It wasn't the least he could do. It was a huge sacrifice, and Rick knew that Terrell was fully aware of how much it was costing Rick. Terrell stood up from the ambulance and held out his hand to shake. Pulling their grasped hands across his heart, Terrell reeled Rick in for a manly hug, slapping him on the back twice.

"Thank you," Terrell said before he set Rick

free from his solid embrace. "I should only need a week. If you can keep her safe for me until then, I should be able to take over from there."

Rick nodded. "Not a problem," he assured Terrell.

Terrell chuckled. "But now you've got to tackle the hard part."

"What's that?" Rick asked.

"Convincing Stephanie to *let* you help her." Terrell shook his head. "I love that girl like my own sister, but she is stubborn and she won't enjoy being needy. She has been the rock of her family for a long time, and no one has ever looked out for her. Don't take it personally if she isn't too keen on the idea of having a bodyguard."

Val walked over and joined the men, balancing Haddie on her hip. "Hey." Her eyebrows pinched together as she made eye contact with Rick. "Have you guys seen Stephanie?" she asked. "I can't find her."

"Yeah, she's waiting by my…" Rick pointed at his car, but she wasn't there. Axle sat on the sidewalk in front of it, but Stephanie was gone. The hairs on the back of his neck raised.

"Axle, *hier*," Rick called Axle to come to him. The dog trotted to his side obediently. Rick patted Axle's saddle area. Axle had been sitting by the car and Stephanie the whole time. If something malicious had happened to Stephanie, he would have alerted Rick. Where was she?

Rick started toward his car with Terrell, Val and Axle following him, but the paramedic called out to Terrell. "Sir, you really need to keep that mask on, and I think we're ready to transport your son to the hospital."

Terrell and Val froze. Their dark complexions paled with worry. Both of their gazes flitted between the ambulance and Rick's patrol car.

Rick put a hand on Terrell's shoulder. "Go!" he commanded. "This is part of what I just volunteered to do. You take care of your family. I'll take care of Stephanie."

It had taken him two hours to find her, and he was not happy. He wanted to chew her out for being so stupid, but finding her on her knees in the front of the church sanctuary dissolved his anger. Well, it dissolved it a little bit. Seeing her alone and praying tugged at his compassion. He was relieved that she was alive and well and not floating upside down near the Ballard docks as Hale's other victims had been. But he was still plenty angry with her. What had she been thinking, taking off like that with nothing more than a note to explain? Didn't her friends deserve better than that?

And why did he care so much? The smart thing would be to leave her right where she was to fend for herself. He had already gone above and beyond what duty dictated. Where had his objectivity gone? Victims had a right to refuse help. But this victim mattered a lot to Val and Terrell, and they mattered too much to Rick to let them down. Like it or not, he was involved for their sake.

Rick crossed his arms and called out down the church aisle, "So are you planning to make me chase you all over this city today, or what?"

Stephanie scrambled up from the front altar and spun to face him. Her body was set to run or fight, and her face was so pale he almost felt guilty for startling her like that. *Almost.*

He raised his hands and stepped closer so she could see him. "Hey. Calm down. It's just me."

Stephanie closed her eyes and relaxed, letting out an audible sigh. Her eyebrows crinkled together. "How'd you find me?"

"The question should be why I had to go looking for you again in the first place. Wasn't saving you once today enough?"

She squared her shoulders. "Terrell would have insisted that I stay with them." She crossed her own arms, mirroring Rick's stance, holding her ground. "They don't need to babysit me, Rick, and sticking around gave Julian opportunity to hurt them more than he already had. Making everyone mad at me was a small price to pay to keep them all safe."

He admired her selflessness, but her actions were still foolish. The minute she'd walked away from the crowd, she had allowed herself to be an easy target. He took a step closer to her. "You could have asked me for help. Terrell and I were setting up a plan for your protection."

"As a favor to Terrell, right?" Her jaw tightened. "I am not your responsibility, Rick. I've always taken care of myself. I'm trying to figure out how to keep doing that."

He had made a promise to Terrell. Now he needed to convince Stephanie to let him fulfill it. "Lone ranger tactics get people killed, Stephanie. Even the toughest cops call for backup."

As soon as he said it, memories flashed, and in his mind he was instantly back on the sidewalk by the warehouse in the Industrial District on the night that he and Axle had been stabbed. He was once again in the dark, rain falling on his face while he waited for either rescue or death, unable to move, unable to do anything but wait for backup to save him.

Most of all he remembered the blood. *Blood on the man's chest where Rick's bullets had entered. Axle's blood. Rick's blood.* And he remembered the sounds. *Sirens. Pounding feet of his backup finally arriving, running to help. Shouts of "Officer down. Officer down."*

Rick shook his head to clear it, returning to the present. "I understand not wanting to be in need of help, believe me, I get that better than you know. But can't you see that taking off on your own and refusing their help has made you more of a burden for Val and Terrell? You should see how worried they are about you right now."

Her face was turned up toward his, and he noticed how close they had moved to each other as they talked. Even in the dim lighting of the sanctuary, he was near enough to see her eyes change to a different shade of blue as they filled with tears. Her head dropped, and she slid her hands up into her hairline and grabbed at her roots. "Ugh. That was not what I was trying to do."

He reached out and pulled her hands down to her sides. "I know it wasn't what you wanted to do, but Stephanie, it took me only two hours to find you in the city. It could have been Hale who found you instead of me. What was your plan?"

She plopped down onto the nearest seat. She rested her head on the back of the chair and stared up at the ceiling. "I didn't have a plan," she admitted, but added, "Yet. I was going to figure it out, maybe find a women's shelter or something that would help me. But once I started walking, I didn't know where to go. I thought about going back to the school to get the stuff I had left there, or going home and making some phone calls. But I was too scared to go to any of the places Julian knew about so I ended up here. Our pastor is meeting with the worship team upstairs, and he said I could hang out here for a while and pray."

She rolled her head to the side in order to look in his direction. "So how did you find me?"

Rick shrugged, then sat down on the chair next to her. "Not sure. Just knew you would want to feel safe and thought your church might be a place you'd go in search of help."

"Yeah, I thought someone would be here and that maybe the office would have a flier or a phone number for a shelter or something." She laughed. "But as silly as it is to say out loud, I also kind of hoped maybe a killer wouldn't want to come into God's house, like church was home base or something."

She sat up and turned toward Rick. She curled one leg under her on the seat and shifted to face him. "I'm really sorry, Rick. About making you hunt me down again. I figured you would be done trying to save me if I didn't want to be saved."

"It's tempting," he told her, even though his anger had fizzled out. He understood her thinking. "But I owe Terrell more than I will ever be able to pay back in this lifetime, so if being your personal bodyguard for a little bit frees him up and eases his mind, that's what I'm going to do."

During the long months of fighting off infection and suffering through rehab, throughout all of the boring hours of being a desk jockey on light duty, all he had cared about was getting back to doing real police work. And now after only one day back at it, he was volunteering to walk away from it again. This girl better be worth it. Apparently she was to Val and Terrell, and they were definitely worth it to him. He couldn't think of any of his other friends who would be able to call in a favor like this.

Stephanie bumped her shoulder against his. "That is if I *let* you be my bodyguard." She was teasing now. Was she giving in?

"Terrell asked for one week to get organized. After that you guys can make whatever other plans you want to make." Rick waited for an answer. "So, think you can put up with me for a week, or do I have to keep hunting you down all night? It's been a long day and I wouldn't mind clocking out and getting something to eat."

She bit her bottom lip. He could tell it was hard for her to admit she didn't have any other options. Then she smiled a real smile like the one in the photograph. She held her hands up in surrender. "Okay. You win. What's the plan?"

SIX

Stephanie inserted the key and unlocked the dead bolt. Her front door was dingy and in need of a clean coat of paint. It routinely stuck, requiring her to slam her shoulder against it to get it loose. The groaning sound the door always made as it slowly swung open sounded to Stephanie as if it were whining in a proper English accent, *Really? Again? Is this* quite *necessary?* Typically, she would tell it to stop being lazy and to quit whining, but she doubted Rick Powell had the scope of imagination necessary to understand her having a conversation with her front door.

When she had left the house earlier that afternoon, she hadn't expected to be bringing home company. Especially not company that made her as nervous as Rick did. What condition had she left everything? Was there anything embarrassing left out that she wouldn't want him to see? She lived what most would consider a minimalist lifestyle in preparation for Liberia, so it shouldn't be too messy. Still, she couldn't help but wonder what her little duplex would look like through Rick's eyes.

Before she stepped over the threshold, Rick pulled her back. She jumped at the sight of his drawn gun. "Let me go ahead of you. I want to clear it first." He gave Axle a command sending him in the door before them.

He was going to search her whole house? Now she had more than just breakfast dishes left out to worry about. "Um, I was hoping to clear it first myself," she said. She gave him a crooked smile. "Don't look too closely, okay?"

Rick's dimple flashed and he winked. "No promises."

Stephanie trailed behind him, her heart racing. Rick's vigilance reminded her that nowhere was safe anymore, not even her own home. Although small, old and quirky, it was cheap, and she loved it. It always felt good to be home, but now tainted by her fear, it felt different and foreign.

"All clear." Rick returned to the kitchen with Axle at his heels and holstered his weapon.

With the threat of a bogeyman jumping out at her gone, Stephanie scanned the house. There were a few dirty dishes on the counter, a basket of laundry to fold on the couch and a mess of papers surrounding her open laptop on her kitchen table. Nothing too embarrassing, but now what was she supposed to do with him?

"Can I get you something? Tea? Coffee?"

"No, thanks. I can entertain myself while you pack." Rick sat down on the couch and the basket of laundry tipped against him.

Stephanie rushed to rescue it before it spilled into his lap. "I am so sorry."

Axle lay down at Rick's feet but cocked his head at her as if he were trying to figure her out. Stephanie had grown up in a house of women. What was she going to do for a whole week with a man and his dog? If she didn't get over her nervousness around them, it was going to be a long, awkward week.

"Well, make yourselves at home. I'm sorry I don't have a TV." She set the laundry basket down behind the couch. "I'll try not to be too long. What am I packing for exactly?"

Rick's gear squeaked as he shifted on the couch to look back at her. He looked so uncomfortable sitting in his uniform with its bulky gun belt. "There's a safe house the US marshals keep near Lake Union. One of our detectives worked out a deal for us to use it for the week. It's a two-bedroom hotel suite that's kind of like a mini-apartment. Just pack whatever clothes and personal items you want, and maybe a few books or movies or something to keep from getting too bored."

A knock on the front door interrupted them. Rick and Axle both sprang up, alert. "You expecting anyone?" Rick asked, drawing his gun again.

Stephanie shook her head.

"Get down behind the couch while I answer it." She shoved the laundry basket aside and squatted down, not liking that she couldn't see what was happening. She strained to hear, then peeked out around the bottom of the couch to watch.

Rick looked through the peephole, then inched open the door. "Can I help you?"

A voice Stephanie didn't recognize answered. "Delivery for, uh…" The voice stalled, probably looking at an address. "Stephanie O'Brien. She live here?" It sounded like a man in his late teens, maybe early twenties, and his nervous tone also sounded like he wasn't expecting a cop to answer the door. She wanted to get a look at him but she didn't dare move out that far from behind the couch.

"Who's it from?" Rick asked him.

"I'm just the delivery boy for the courier company. I don't know anything about the packages or where they come from."

"You're delivering on a Saturday?"

"Twenty-four/seven. Keeps our company competitive with the big guys." The poor kid sounded so nervous, Stephanie felt sorry for him.

Rick grilled him a little bit more, asking for his name and the courier company's name and address, until he finally let the poor guy off the hook.

"What is it?" Stephanie asked, standing up as he closed the door.

In his hand, Rick held a large manila envelope. He placed it down on her kitchen table just as his cell phone rang. "Hey, Gary. What's up?"

Stephanie fingered the envelope. What was it? Dread mixed with curiosity. Was it from -Julian?

She turned the envelope around in her hand, examining it. She found no return address, of course, only her name and her own address chicken-scratched out on the front in blue ink. The envelope looked harmless enough. She peeked at Rick. His back was turned toward her as he spoke to someone on his cell.

Curiosity won out, and because she knew Rick would probably stop her from doing it, she sliced the top open and dumped the contents into her hand before he got off the phone and stopped her. She had to know what was inside.

Rick ended his phone call. "Does the word *anthrax* mean nothing to you?"

But Stephanie wasn't listening to his words; she was too captivated by the stack of photos that had fallen out of the envelope. There were pictures of several of her students leaving school for the day; there was a picture of Joash wearing his backpack running into his school, another of Val and Haddie out shopping, and others of Terrell at work. There were shots of her church, of her pastor and of Stephanie standing outside talking with some of the women from her Bible study. There were photos taken from her sister's Liberia blog showing Emily and Ty, and many of the kids from the orphanage that Stephanie loved. There was even a photo of her mother in front of the casino. Had he gone to Oregon to find her? Picture after picture revealed a location she frequented or a person connected to her.

She reached the final photo. It was a shot taken outside of the Watkinses' house fire earlier that day. In the picture, Rick was draping the blanket over her shoulders and the camera lens had zoomed in on the look of tender concern he had on his face. Scrawled across the corner of the picture in black permanent marker were the words, "Awww, how sweet."

Rick reached out his hand. "Let me see."

Stephanie handed him the stack. "Rick, if I

care about someone, their picture is in there. He didn't leave anyone out." She could hear her own panic.

Then she handed him the note that came with the photos in the envelope. In the same chicken-scratch handwriting, the sender had written: *You can run, but can* they *hide?*

It had to be Julian Hale.

Rick flipped the last photo over, examining the back. "These pictures came from the one-hour at Walmart. We can look into their security cameras, but we already know who they're from. Let's not touch them anymore, and I'll send them to the lab to be fingerprinted. But for now, we've got another more pressing problem."

SEVEN

Stephanie wondered what could possibly be bigger than this threat, but she asked, anyway, "What problem?"

"That was Gary Shelton on the phone. He's the head detective on this case, and he's been going through all of the stuff we found at Hale's house today." Rick paused, turning in circles, searching for something. "Gary called to warn us that he can see us."

"What did he mean, he can see us?"

"He meant what he said. Gary is on Hale's personal computer right now, and..." Rick reached across the kitchen table and slammed her laptop closed. "We better hope Hale doesn't have one of those with him with the same software as his home computer, because Gary was looking *through* this and seeing *us*."

She shook her head, refusing to believe it. "No way." She backed away from the table. "No way." She would not accept that Julian Hale had been spying on her in her own home. For how long? What had he seen?

"How?"

Rick pointed at her closed laptop. "Do you have a webcam on that?"

"Yes. I video chat with my sister on it." Nausea rolled. The violation she felt was indescribable. "I think I'm going to be sick."

"I know this is hard, but we don't have time to deal with it. If he was monitoring your house remotely, he knows we are here. We need to move and somehow avoid being followed."

He's been watching me. Where else? At school, too? He's threatened everyone. Everyone. There had been too many blows today. She looked at her couch situated in front of the little gas fireplace. She wanted to quit, to wrap up in a quilt with a cup of tea on her couch and process all that had hit her in such a short time. But Rick was right. She needed to act, not think. Once they were in the safe house, there would be plenty of time to think.

"Okay."

"There's no way to know what other technology he has messed with. Don't pack anything that he could trace. Leave your phone here. Don't bring your laptop or a tablet."

"I can't leave my phone." She held up the

stack of photos. "I need my contact list to call these people to warn them."

"Just leave it. We're going to the police department. I can help you contact your friends from there."

Axle circled Rick's feet, most likely assuming Rick's agitation meant it was work time. It fascinated her how quickly Axle transformed from a playful puppy to an intense animal who seemed human in his desire to work with his partner. She was beginning to love that dog.

"Stephanie?" Rick was pacing, and rubbing his palms together. She looked up from Axle to Rick, expecting more instructions. Instead, he waved a hand toward her bedroom door. "Hurry."

Five minutes later, Stephanie handed him a duffel bag.

"That's it?" Rick asked, sounding shocked.

"I've got enough clothes and a toiletry bag. What else do I need?"

"No complaints here," he assured her. "My experience with women made me expect three rolling suitcases and a gigantic bathroom bag."

"I travel light," she told him. *His experience with women?* A stab of jealousy hit her. She began to imagine his past girlfriends, wondering what they looked like and why he hadn't ever been married. He must have a reason for still being single. *Stop it, Stephanie. More important things to focus on at the moment.*

Rick's hand found her back and guided her toward the front door. Before he opened it, he said, "Go for the car as quickly as possible."

They rushed down her front stoop to Rick's waiting car. Stephanie ducked in while Rick kenneled Axle and tossed her bag into the back. The whole process from front door to pulling away from the curb had taken less than two minutes.

Rick's headlights reflected off the wet streets. Stephanie noted that the night sky had finally caught up with her sense of the length of this day. It felt so much later than only eight o'clock. Was constantly running her new reality? Would she forever be dodging the balls Julian threw at her, or was there hope of being free of him? *Lord, please let them catch him. I don't want to live like this forever.*

"Where are we going?" she asked Rick.

"To the department to meet with Gary Shelton," he said, looking into the rearview mirror. "I don't want to risk Hale following us to the hotel. Gary wants to talk with you, and I need to go home to change and pack. Gary will transport you to the safe house, and I'll meet you there."

Stephanie blinked. Rick was leaving her

alone at the police department? She picked at a hangnail while he explained his plan. It made sense—the last thing she needed was Julian knowing where she was hiding—but the idea of separating from Rick made her nervous.

Rick entered a security code, and a gate clicked open, allowing them to enter the department parking lot. Stephanie breathed easy for the first time since leaving her house. She had never seen so many police cars in one place. A fleet of vehicles backed into their parking spaces looked like an army ready to go when called. Julian couldn't get in here. Where could she be safer than locked behind fences surrounded by cops? Maybe she should move in here to hide from Julian. She could find some unused storage room out of the way and hole up until he was arrested.

That helps you, but what about your friends? She would love to forget, even if for only five minutes, how much was really at stake.

Inside, Rick led her through a maze of cubicles until they came to a messy desk where an older man sat. He rose to greet them. "Aw, here's our girl," he said.

His dark eyes and full brows contrasted dramatically with his receding salt-and-pepper hair. He appeared to be in his fifties, but he exuded an energy Stephanie didn't usually see even in men much younger than him. The marathon race number and medal he had framed and hanging on his cubicle wall explained why.

He extended his hand to Stephanie. "Gary Shelton. You have no idea how glad I am to see you safe, young lady." The lines surrounding his sad eyes made her believe he had seen his share of *unsafe* young ladies. Goose bumps ran up her arms at the thought.

"Thank you," Stephanie said. She glanced at Rick and added, "I'm glad to *be* safe."

"Detective Shelton is leading our investigation on this case," Rick explained to Stephanie and then asked the other man, "Anything new?"

The detective handed Rick a folder. "This is the updated FBI profile report."

Rick's eyebrows furrowed as he scanned the report he held in his hands. Stephanie hoped he would hand it to her next. She wanted to know everything she could about Julian, to understand why he had targeted her like this, but giving her access to an FBI report probably wasn't going to happen.

Rick looked up from the file and asked Shelton, "What about those other three photographs I saw in his attic?"

"They were out-of-state victims that we didn't know about," Shelton told him. "I've been on the phone all day with other departments connecting the dots."

The detective pointed to a map he had pinned to his cubicle wall. "Lora Johnson, 35, Saint Paul, Minnesota." Then he moved his finger to a different location and said, "Kelly Halloway, 32, and Naomi Folsom, 25, both from Milwaukee, Wisconsin." He dropped his arm to his side as if it were suddenly too heavy. "Hale grew up in a suburb of Saint Paul and went to school with Johnson. Before moving to Seattle, he worked for a tech company in Milwaukee. There will be a solid case against him once we bring him in."

"Same MO?" Rick asked.

Stephanie caught the questioning look the detective shot Rick. "It's okay," she assured him. "Don't water it down for me. I need to know the truth."

Shelton gave a curt nod before he responded, "Final cause of death for all six was strangulation and…" His gaze flitted back to Stephanie before he added, "All six victims were educators of some form."

Stephanie stepped back, shocked. "Julian is killing teachers?"

"Yes. Lora Johnson was a high school computer applications teacher in Saint Paul, and the other two taught together at a school in Milwaukee. The Seattle victims were a preschool teacher, another high school teacher and a tutor at a learning center."

Rick read out loud from the profile report in his hands, "The suspect is likely a white male in his late thirties, early forties. He is likely motivated by a need for power and dominance stemming from early childhood feelings of helplessness after suffering abuse at the hands of a male authority figure. The victimization of educators is most likely the result of a perceived failed romantic relationship or personal rejection from a member of that demographic."

He stopped reading and asked Shelton, "That first victim, Lora Johnson?"

"It looks like she paid the ultimate price for spurning his love, and all the rest were guilty of reminding him of her," Shelton said.

"Why me?" Stephanie asked the detective. "I mean besides being a teacher like the other women, why did he choose me? I thought I was always kind to him. I can't think of anything I did or said to make him hate me like this."

"It isn't anything you did to him that motivates him, it is simply who you are." Shelton nodded toward the file Rick held. "You fit his profile. You are young, and although you have friends, you are basically alone in the city with no immediate family connections in the area. He saw you as an easy target. Julian Hale is a systematic and patient killer. He targets people he thinks will be easy to capture, but then he takes his time getting to know them, knowing their routines and their friends. He becomes obsessed."

"Let me show you something." The detective beckoned Stephanie and Rick over to a computer on his desk. "This is the computer we took from Hale's property today." He tapped the screen and asked Stephanie, "Recognize this place?"

Both Rick and Stephanie leaned toward the screen, eager to get a look. Stephanie leaned in even farther, squinting at the grainy images, looking for clues that would tell her what was on the screen. She felt warmth radiating from Rick as he leaned across her back, straining to get a look at the computer over the top of her head.

Stephanie grimaced. She knew exactly what place the camera was recording. "My classroom," she spat out.

She turned her back to the computer. She was done looking at it. First her home, now her classroom—how dare Julian desecrate her safe places? She rubbed her arms, trying to wipe away the thought of Julian's eyes spying on her.

The detective turned his chair to face her and then sat down. He leaned on his knees, looking at his feet instead of making eye contact with her. "Hale doesn't strike until he is sure of his success," Shelton said. "He hasn't left room for error in the past."

He sat back up. "But you have one advantage the others don't have."

"What's that?" Stephanie asked him.

"You are alive."

He reached up and touched her arm. "You are the one that got away. We know who he is now, and we got to you before he did."

Stephanie sat down in a chair by the cubicle wall. "But he's threatened everyone I care about. I'm alive, but are the people I love safe?" She felt Rick's reassuring hand on her shoulder and appreciated his strong grip.

Detective Shelton crossed his arms and leaned back in his chair again. "I know you are worried about your friends, but for now I'm pretty sure you are Hale's primary target. I've been studying this case for over a year, and my guess is he has fixated on you, not your friends. The threats today are just a way to scare you and prove to you once again that he is in control. For now, your safety has to be your top priority. And ours."

"My priority is seeing him caught. I want to be free, and I want the people I love safe. I'm not going to be content sitting around in hiding for long." Stephanie leaned back in her chair and crossed her own arms, trying to appear bigger than her five-foot-three frame. Somehow she needed to get them to stop seeing her as a fragile thing about to break, and convince them to focus on the bigger picture. "I don't know a lot about Julian, but I know some. I've got to be able to help somehow. Can't you use me as bait or something?"

Gary Shelton smiled up at Rick. "I like this girl." Then he patted Stephanie's arm before rolling his chair away from her. "For now we focus on getting you two into hiding without Hale knowing your location. Rick will go home in a different car than he came in. We'll put you in a disguise and take you out of here in a separate car. Once we're sure there's no tail, we'll meet Rick at the marshals' hotel suite."

"Thanks, Gary," Rick said, shaking the detective's hand. To Stephanie he said, "See you soon."

When Rick was out of earshot, the detective turned back to Stephanie. "Get a good night's sleep. Lie low for a few days and let the dust settle." He put a hand on her shoulder. "Then I just might take you up on that offer."

Later that night, Rick tossed in the grip of a nightmare. Against the backdrop of a dark Seattle industrial complex, Stephanie begged him to help her as Julian Hale backed her into a corner, swinging a gigantic knife. Rain ran into Rick's eyes, his mouth, choking him and drenching his clothing. He was frozen. He couldn't move to help Stephanie. He could only stand and listen to her screams, watching as helplessness enveloped him.

The clicking of the hotel heater turning on woke him up. He was soaked with sweat and his heart raced. *It's just the dream again.* Different versions of the same nightmare had played out for over a year now. The dream's setting never changed. It was always the same dark, rainy exterior of the warehouse where he and Axle had been attacked and stabbed, but somehow the old dream had adapted to his new reality by including Stephanie and Julian Hale. He breathed deeply, trying to slow his heart and orient himself with the unfamiliar room he had woken up in.

He remembered he was in the hotel safe house, but beyond that there was something that was still off, something that didn't feel right. What was it? The bed was so cold and empty. He patted around the sheets. Where was Axle?

After the stabbing, Axle had assigned himself as Rick's personal bodyguard. Apparently Axle's guard duty included protecting Rick while he slept, as well. Training him to do otherwise had been an exercise in futility. Rick often thought, *Good thing I'm not married.* Instead of a wife, he always awoke to Axle snoring next to him with his left paw covering his chest protectively. The dog was the most loyal partner ever. But where was he now?

Rick slipped out of the covers and grabbed his pistol out of the nightstand. He searched the living room and kitchenette space of the suite. Axle was nowhere to be found. Stephanie's bedroom door was cracked open slightly. Should he check on her, or was that invading her privacy too much?

Saturday had been such a long day for her, and they hadn't gotten settled into the suite until after midnight. He hoped she was fast asleep, forgetting all the fear of the day before. The microwave in the kitchenette said it was only five in the morning. He didn't want to disturb her, but with Axle MIA, he needed to make sure she was okay. Rick pushed on the door and peeked inside.

Stephanie was sound asleep on her back under the covers, her strawberry blond curls splayed out around her like a halo. She looked so peaceful. Next to her was a sleeping Axle, his left paw draped over her protectively. Axle lifted one eyelid, then promptly closed it again as if to say, *Go away, you're interrupting my beauty sleep.*

"Traitor," Rick whispered.

Stephanie sat straight up in bed and gasped. Rick jumped back behind the door. *Wow. Light sleeper.* Maybe her sleep wasn't as peaceful as he thought.

Rick peeked around the door, feeling guilty. "Sorry. Don't wake up. I just couldn't find Axle. Looks like he thought you needed his company more than I did."

Stephanie squinted her eyes, looking so cute in her confusion. She glanced from Rick in the doorway to Axle on the bed and then smiled. She patted Axle and then said in a hoarse voice, "Thanks for looking out for me, pal." Axle yawned his noisy response.

"Want me to get him off?" Rick asked her.

Stephanie lay back down on her pillow. "Not unless you miss him too much."

"Go back to sleep," Rick whispered, and closed her door.

Back in his own bed, Rick couldn't sleep. He would never admit it to anyone, but he did miss Axle's company. And if he was continuing with the honesty, he also wished he had someone special in his life. But the scar across his belly, the nightmares and the memories of Allie walking away all reminded him why that was a life he couldn't have. The sooner he accepted that he wasn't Terrell Watkins, the better off he would be. It was good to manage his expectations.

He tossed and turned until he finally threw off the comforter and swung his legs over the edge of the bed. *I give up.* After taking a quick shower and dressing, Rick wandered into the kitchenette and found the coffeepot. He could hear Stephanie's shower running. The coffee aroma was just beginning to hit his nose when she emerged from her room.

"I'm sorry I woke you up," he told her.

She shook her head and started scrunching her damp curls between her hands. "It wasn't you. I never can sleep well in a hotel. It's too noisy."

On cue, the sounds of rolling suitcases passed by their front door. Above their heads, water ran through the pipes. Someone upstairs must be showering, too. Rick had to agree with her, it was noisy.

"Breakfast?" he asked. He shuffled through the groceries he had brought with him last night, but nothing looked too appetizing. Stephanie opened the blinds to a predawn view of houseboats and yachts floating on Lake Union. Sunrise peeked a bit from behind a distant hill. The scene looked peaceful and hopeful, not like a city hiding a murderer.

"I've got to give Axle a bathroom break. When we get back up, should we make this feel like a real vacation and order room service?"

She flashed him the grin he was beginning to anticipate. "I'm a sucker for breakfast," she said. "It's my favorite meal."

"Then it's a deal." He liked making her happy, especially when she rewarded him with that gorgeous smile.

"Can I go outside with you guys?" she asked him, a hopeful look on her face. "I'd love to get some fresh air."

Frowning, he said, "Better not."

How quickly they had moved from his being able to make her smile to having to tell her no. "Until we are sure we weren't followed last night, I'm afraid you're stuck in here," he explained.

Disappointment flashed on her face, but she replaced it quickly with a look of resolve and said, "I understand."

Rick hated that she had to be a virtual prisoner in this hotel room, but he couldn't risk taking her out in the open. "Shelton has a security detail set up in the hotel. They've got an officer on his way to stay with you until Axle and I get back up here."

Having a strange cop standing guard in the room would make her feel even more like a prisoner, but it couldn't be helped, and Axle was pacing by the door.

He gave her what he hoped was an apologetic smile. "We'll be quick, and then we'll get that breakfast I promised you."

Outside, Rick kept catching himself glancing up at the fifth floor of the hotel. He was feeling so antsy. Someone else was doing his job. Having a security detail to monitor the hotel and spell him as he needed made sense, of course, but being apart from Stephanie unsettled him. Axle wanted to play, but Rick cut it short. He couldn't get back to the room fast enough, and when he dismissed the other officer, he saw a look of relief cross Stephanie's face, too. It felt good to know she was getting comfortable with him, or that at least he made her feel safe.

He called down their breakfast order right away, but it felt like an eternity passed before they finally heard a knock at the door.

"Room service."

Stephanie's stomach growled so loud, Rick heard it. "Ah, I can smell it," she said, giggling.

Rick opened the door and found the covered tray waiting on the floor. She was right, it did smell incredible. Axle squeezed past Rick into the hallway, barking loudly at the tray in Rick's hands.

"Axle, *pfui*!" *Stop that!* Rick nudged Axle back into the room with his knee, but the dog wouldn't shut up. "*Pfui!* Are you trying to get us kicked out of the hotel, dog? Be quiet."

The dog didn't like it, but he obeyed, replacing the barking with a much quieter whine as he paced.

Stephanie wriggled forward on the red microfiber couch as Rick placed the tray on the coffee table in front of her. "Madam, as you requested," he said.

Stephanie shut her eyes and inhaled. "Yum. Val's dinner was so long ago, I'm starving." She turned a sympathetic face toward the dog. "Sorry to eat in front of you, Axle. I'll share," she promised him.

Rick's stomach growled, too. "He's fine. He knows better than to beg like that."

Axle barked sharply. He was picking up bad manners.

Stephanie reached over and lifted the cover off two steaming plates of golden pancakes. The pats of butter had melted to perfection. Rick stared at the tray, precious seconds ticking away as *something is wrong* needled his brain. It took about three seconds to register what his eyes were seeing.

An antique-style alarm clock sat between the two plates. Rick saw the blast cap, the wires and the large bundle of dynamite.

He grabbed Stephanie's wrist and yanked her off the couch, shoving her forward.

"Run!" He pushed her out the door, praying every footstep would take them far enough away.

EIGHT

It took Stephanie several seconds for her mind to catch up to her running feet. There had been a bomb on the breakfast tray. She had seen it with her own eyes. *A bomb.*

The hotel was laid out in a crescent shape with several floors of open balconies overlooking a central patio-style courtyard. Unsuspecting guests filled the courtyard below where they ate breakfast, read their newspapers and drank coffee, oblivious to the bomb about to explode in the fifth-floor suite above their heads. The same bomb that could detonate behind Stephanie's back at any moment. Her leg muscles twitched. She needed to run away.

Rick hung over the balcony. "There's a bomb," he bellowed. A few people stared up at him in shock, a few pointed up at him, probably wondering what that crazy person was yelling about up there.

"Evacuate the building!" Rick screamed once

more and then gave up. Stephanie and Axle followed him. They couldn't waste time waiting to see if anyone acted on Rick's warning or not. *Please let people hear him; let them get out before it goes off.*

Dialing his cell as he ran, Rick breathlessly relayed the news to Shelton and then screamed yet another warning to two businessmen in suits waiting by the elevator ahead of them. When they heard Rick's words, they dropped their bags and ran.

Sweat trickled down Stephanie's neck under her hair. Would Rick's warning reach anyone else in time? Who would get hurt when the bomb detonated?

A door opened into the hallway, and a woman holding a baby carrier stepped in front of them. The woman's other hand clasped the hand of a toddler. The little boy's eyes widened at the sight of the crazy people and the dog running toward his little family.

Stephanie slowed her running and shuddered. *Lord, no! Not babies.* Her lungs burned. Gasping to regain her breath, she managed to yell at the woman, "There's a bomb! Get them out of here! Run!"

The woman froze with a deer-in-the-headlights gaze. Stephanie estimated at least three minutes had passed. When would the explosion hit them? They were wasting precious seconds.

"Run!" Stephanie screamed at her again. "Get your kids away from here."

The woman snapped awake and ran a few slow steps with the cumbersome baby carrier, dragging the toddler behind her before she stopped and sobbed, "But my husband's in the shower. We were just getting breakfast."

Stephanie scooped up the little boy, while Rick said, "Keep running, I'll get your husband."

"Rick, no," Stephanie protested. *Save yourself. I need you with me.*

"Go. Get those kids as far away as you can." Rick pounded his flat palm against the door where the family had emerged. "Police! Open the door!" He was still pounding and yelling as Stephanie and the woman continued down the hall.

Every fiber in her being fought against abandoning Rick, but Stephanie couldn't listen to her instincts. Silent tears streamed down her cheeks as she left him. They had to get these babies to safety. It was probably already too late.

As they reached the stairwell, the wailing screams and flashing strobe lights of the hotel's alarm system kicked in. Shelton must have warned the front desk. Stephanie was grateful for the blaring warning. The more time that passed before the bomb went off meant more people would hear it and get out safely, and the fewer injuries or deaths she would have on her conscience.

Doors slammed as people abandoned their rooms, shoving past the two slower-moving women and children on the stairs. Stephanie winced at every noise or touch, but if the bomb hadn't detonated already, would it at all? So much time had gone by already, maybe the bomb was a dud, just Julian's idea of a joke.

Axle whizzed by her legs, running down the stairs several floors, and then circling back. He barked at her and repeated the same cycle over and over, urging the two women to hurry. The toddler screamed in Stephanie's ear, squirming and reaching for his mother. Stephanie's arms were sweaty and slippery. She was afraid she might drop the boy if he kept moving like that.

"Sit still, sweetie. I'll give you to your mom when we're outside, okay?" His poor mother stumbled behind Stephanie several times. Running down steep stairs while juggling a heavy baby carrier at the same time didn't look like an easy task.

"You're okay, Max," the woman yelled to her son. "Be a good boy."

Other people rushed past them on the stairs,

slowing their progress even further. It felt like the entire hotel full of people was attempting an escape down this one tight stairwell.

They were almost to the ground floor when the woman stopped, red-faced and heaving for air. She knelt and started unlatching the straps securing her baby. "I'm going to take her out of the carrier. Keep going."

Not wanting to leave her, Stephanie stopped and said, "Hurry."

Then she heard more running footsteps above them, and a male voice called out, "Marla, I'm coming."

A man in boxers and a damp T-shirt ran barefoot around the corner, grabbing the baby from his wife. Marla turned to Stephanie and reached for her son.

Stephanie handed the boy to his mother. Stretching up on tiptoes, she peered around the couple and up the stairs behind them. "Where's Rick?" she asked Marla's husband. "Why isn't he with you?"

But Stephanie never got her answer. An explosive shock wave hit her first, knocking her to her knees, erasing all doubt of the bomb's authenticity. The lights flickered for a second and then a heavy *boom* sound echoed down the stairwell, sending vibrations right through Stephanie's bones. Marla and her husband flung themselves over their children. Stephanie covered her ears and huddled against the wall. Warm fur blanketed her as Axle positioned himself close around her body, ever her vigilant protector.

"Rick," she screamed. "Rick!" She squeezed her eyes shut and pulled into a fetal position.

Then a strong arm wrapped around her shoulders, pulling her in, and she heard Rick's voice speaking in her ear. "I'm right here."

A sense of déjà vu settled on Stephanie as she and Rick watched the commotion from the edge of the crowd gathered in the hotel parking lot. It was her third experience in two days of watching a bunch of emergency responders cleaning up a mess that Julian Hale had made.

Axle was thirsty and hungry, so when another K-9 officer offered to get him some food and water and to kennel the dog in his patrol car, Rick thanked him and handed him the leash. Then he began pointing out the different agencies and command staff to Stephanie, helping her to understand what she was seeing. Police officers, SWAT, FBI, ATF, paramedics and firefighters swarmed around them. He pointed to a tall man in a tailored suit with silver hair and a trimmed gray goatee. "There's the mayor."

"Looks like a good time to rob a bank," she

said, her eyes wide in awc of the response. "Is *everyone* here?"

"We don't take a bomb going off in our city lightly."

They had been told that a hotel employee—the same one who had left the kitchen with their room service order—had been found unconscious in a utility closet. That meant Julian had delivered the bomb himself. Was he still close by? Stephanie imagined him hiding somewhere in the bushes watching the scene, thrilled by the chaos and mess he had created. She wondered if the huge scale of descending law enforcement and media attention delighted him. Did this enormous response, along with the heightened human emotion, feed his sickness? Would it fuel him on to bigger and better things than chasing after an unimportant schoolteacher?

The entire block had been cordoned off, and all area buildings had been evacuated. Police were escorting curious pedestrians outside of the crime-scene tape, and refusing to comment to all of the members of the media who were leaning across the barricades crying out for information.

Clumps of people stood by the barricades and answered the reporters' questions, eager for their fifteen minutes of fame. How soon until the reporters figured out Stephanie and Rick's connection with the explosion? She spotted an attractive blonde woman wearing a blue parka with a Channel 4 News patch on its sleeve. It was Kristine Scott, the news anchor Stephanie watched every night before bed, and she was interviewing one of the men Stephanie and Rick had warned outside the elevator. Stephanie averted her eyes and stepped behind a large pillar to hide from his view before he recognized her and pointed her out to the newswoman.

Rick draped his arm around her shoulder and put his lips to her ear so no one else could hear. "Play it cool and try to blend in, but stay alert. Hale could be nearby. Shelton is on his way with a car to get us out of here, but in the meantime, I don't want a camera or microphone shoved in our faces. The less attention we draw, the better."

Stephanie agreed. She did not want her students' parents turning on the eleven o'clock news and seeing their child's teacher on the screen. Rick guided her behind an ambulance and then farther down a sidewalk. On any other morning this street would be busy with traffic. Today it was empty of cars and eerily silent.

Stephanie had to remind herself to breathe. They had distanced themselves from the crowd and the watchful eyes of the media, but if Julian was out there somewhere paying attention, the new spot also made them more vulnerable to another attack. Maybe they should go back to the parking lot to wait. Without thinking about it, she stepped closer to Rick's side for comfort.

"Shelton will be here any minute," he reassured her. "We need to be ready to jump in when he pulls up. Then we can go get Axle."

The Space Needle stood tall in the skyline on Stephanie's left, the iconic landmark reminding her of how far downtown they were. Over four million people lived in the Seattle area, yet somehow Julian Hale kept zeroing in on their location. He was doing the impossible.

"How is he doing it?" she asked Rick, sensing the same frustration eating at him. "It shouldn't be this hard to hide in a city the size of Seattle." Maybe she and Rick should forget about waiting for Shelton and find their own hiding place. But remembering how well taking off on her own had worked out for her yesterday convinced her that was not a feasible option.

"I don't know," Rick answered her. "We've got to figure it out or it's useless to even try to hide. He's got to be doing more than just following us, but I can't figure out how he's tracking us."

Stephanie stared at the shops across the street that bumped up to Lake Union. There was a chowder restaurant, and a marina selling yachts.

On another day, she would have had fun crossing the street and exploring the shops and luxury boats for sale. But in reality, on a normal Sunday morning like this one, she wouldn't be downtown at all. She would be at church, sitting next to Val. She would probably have Haddie cuddled up on her lap and Joash snuggled next to her side. She wanted to be in that place of safety and contentment instead of standing outside a crime scene investigation knowing that she was the reason for all of this uproar.

Her mind wandered to her school. She imagined the kids climbing off their school buses tomorrow morning, dragging backpacks behind them, and then finding a substitute teacher when they walked in the door. A pang of something like homesickness hit her. She missed her normal routine. She surveyed the chaos surrounding her and pressed her fingers to her lips. *Thank You that all of this happened on a weekend and not while I was at school. Please don't let Julian hurt my kids.*

As soon as she and Rick got to somewhere safe, she needed to call her principal. She had already talked to him, and Detective Shelton had promised to contact him, too, but she needed to reinforce with Jim again just how much danger they could be in at the school. She wouldn't be able to live with one of her kids getting hurt because of her.

Stephanie scanned the crowd behind her trying to assess the damage. Their hotel suite had been completely destroyed in the blast, taking out much of the surrounding rooms, including those above and below theirs. She could see a paramedic working on a woman's hand, and a few people had bleeding cuts on their faces. They must have been hit by flying debris, but so far it didn't look to her that people had been hurt too seriously. Julian had given them all enough time to get out. Why was that?

She turned to Rick and said, "Another thing I don't understand is why it took so long for the bomb to go off." She didn't mean to sound ungrateful for the extra time that had saved so many lives.

"Not that I'm complaining," she corrected herself, "But when we were running, I kept expecting the explosion to happen at any moment. It seemed like it took forever."

"No. I thought the same thing." Rick shuffled his feet and crossed his arms, his biceps stretching the sleeves of his T-shirt. He looked so strong, yet Julian had him perplexed, too. It made the ground beneath Stephanie feel unsteady, as if she were standing on one of the swaying boats moored at the docks across the street.

"I think he was giving us time to get out," Rick said.

"What?" Nothing Julian was doing made any sense to her. There had been so many opportunities for him to kill her already if that was his intent; why did he keep letting her live? "Why bother sending the bomb at all if he wasn't trying to kill us?"

"Remember what Gary Shelton told you? You are the fish that got away. Hale needs to feel in control, to believe he holds all the power. The bomb was just a message. He's telling us that when he is ready to do it, he's going to do it his way."

"By *it*, you mean kill me," Stephanie said.

"That's not going to happen, Stephanie." Rick reached out for her hand and she took it, comforted by the gesture. It was just palm to palm, not as meaningful as if their fingers interlaced, but it wasn't something that two strangers would do. Rick was beginning to feel less like an acquaintance and more like a friend.

"I'm sick of Julian having the upper hand," she said.

"Me, too," Rick agreed. "But you can't let him get inside your head. Otherwise he accomplished exactly what he set out to do. We've had some setbacks, but it is past time for the tide to turn in our favor."

It was strangely peaceful holding Rick's hand and watching the floating boats bobbing in the water across the street. She wished they could get in one of those yachts and sail far, far away from the threat of Julian Hale and all of the fear and guilt he had brought into her life. Getting back to Africa had never sounded better to her. How far would Julian be willing to go before he gave up on her?

Something in the parking lot kitty-corner to where they stood pulled her attention. She squinted to clear her vision. A man stood at the far side of the lot, too far away from her to see him clearly. Hadn't the police already evacuated all of those buildings? He was probably just some looky-lou checking out all the excitement. But the more she stared at him, the more intrigued she became. Instead of looking at the spectacle around the hotel, he seemed to be staring at her instead. He stood abnormally still, with a perfect, erect posture she knew too well. He raised a hand in a wave and Stephanie's insides turned to ice.

"Rick, there he is." Stephanie gasped out the words, scarcely believing he was really standing there and not a figment of her imagination. She dropped Rick's hand and pointed at the man's retreating figure. "Julian Hale is right there across the street."

* * *

"Wait here for Shelton," Rick shouted back to Stephanie.

Pistol in hand, he sprinted across the street and hurdled over low shrubbery into the parking lot on the other side. He wobbled some on his landing, but continued running. He struggled to keep his eye on Hale's head as he weaved between cars. Rick pushed his legs and pumped his arms harder, needing to increase his speed and decrease Hale's significant head start. Rick didn't know how he could ever catch up on foot.

"Stop! Police!" Rick yelled after Hale's retreating form. It was useless. Even if Hale could hear the command, he probably wouldn't obey it.

He needed backup, but he would have lost Hale if he hadn't immediately taken off after him. Rick kept running and grabbed at his cell phone on his belt. In the movies it always looked so easy for the hero to dial a phone, carry on a conversation and continue to pursue the bad guy. It wasn't easy. At all.

Desperate for air, he tried to spit out words to communicate the situation and his location to Shelton without losing sight of Hale. *Where'd he go?*

"You've got to get me some backup," Rick panted. "He had too big of a head start. I've lost sight of him. We've got to stop him before he disappears into the downtown crowd."

Two seconds later, Rick heard the screams of pursuing patrol cars and the shouts of men on foot coming to his aid far behind him. They had to flush Hale out of hiding. Rick didn't think he could stand it if Hale escaped again.

When the parking lot ended, Rick came to a crossroads. He had to decide if Hale would turn into the city or go for the docks. Heading toward the lake was a dead end, but his backup was already searching the streets and no one was searching the boats yet. Rick's instinct sent him sprinting for the docks.

His lungs were on fire. He hadn't run this hard in a long time. All of the rehab he had done during the past year had left him stronger than ever, but his endurance still needed work. If only he hadn't let Randy Mitchell take Axle to his car. He needed his partner with him. Axle would have found Hale by now. Rick imagined the dog sprinting ahead of him, tackling Hale to the ground and ending this whole deal.

Adrenaline surged, pumping strength into his limbs. Visualizing himself capturing Hale and setting Stephanie free of this life of hiding drove Rick forward. He covered ground faster than he thought possible. He spotted a brief flash of movement. Rick's instinct had been right; Hale had gone toward the water instead of downtown. But why? It was a dead end unless he planned on swimming away.

Rick slowed and ducked behind a nearby sign. He raised his gun, his pounding heart contrasting with the serenity of his surroundings. Seagulls circled lazily overhead, chattering to one another as they searched for food. Water lapped a steady rhythm against the gently rocking boats. Then, *crack*.

The gunshot rang out, splintering the peace and sending the gulls squawking. Hale had a gun!

Rick ran down the dock, firing his own gun in response. The pungent scent of seawater and fish filled his nostrils. Images of the night he and Axle were stabbed assaulted his memory. The warehouse where it had happened was only three miles away from these docks, and the same salty smell had been in his nose that night as well. History could not repeat itself here. Rick had fought too hard. He would not allow Julian Hale to take him down again.

Hale dived onto the deck of the nearest yacht, glass shattering from the cabin door where Rick's bullet hit directly above him. Hale popped up and fired back at Rick, but he was an inexperienced shot, unable to hit a moving target.

Rick jumped onboard the boat nearest him

and ripped his cell phone from his belt once again. He rolled to his back and dialed Gary Shelton. "Hale's firing at me, Gary. Where's that backup you promised me?"

"Where are you?"

"Last set of docks before the park. Do you have Stephanie?"

"Yes. Almost to you," Gary shouted into the phone. "Don't lose him."

"Not planning on it." Rick hung up and called down the dock. "Give it up, Hale. You're trapped."

But Hale didn't answer. The silence unsettled Rick as he rolled over and popped up to look again over the edge of the boat. He scanned the dock. Where was Hale hiding now? "My backup will be here any second," Rick shouted. "This is a dead end. Turn yourself in before you make it worse."

But his words flew out to sea, useless. No one was listening.

In his peripheral vision, Rick saw movement. He spun in time to watch Hale sprinting down an adjoining dock. He must have hopped across to a different boat when Rick dropped down on this other yacht. Rick leaped off the boat and ran, jumping from boat to boat until he clambered onto the same dock as the fleeing man. Rick could hear the distant squeal of Gary

Shelton's tires as his car turned into the parking lot behind him, and the screaming sirens of the patrol cars he brought with him. He heard slamming doors, shouting men and stomping boots. He'd have help soon. Would it be soon enough?

Hale reached the end of the dock. "Dead end, Hale," Rick yelled. They both raised their guns and fired at each other simultaneously. As the bullet left his gun, Rick wasn't sure where it struck, but he was certain he had hit Hale somewhere.

He tried to raise his gun to fire again, but his hadn't been the only bullet to find its target. One of Hale's bullets had sliced across Rick's shoulder. Searing white pain erupted across his brain. Rick heard the splash of Hale's body hitting the water. Had he killed him?

With his right arm hanging limp at his side, Rick launched himself forward, willing back the black edges of pain threatening to take him under. It wasn't until he was going down himself that Rick realized he had tripped on a knotted piece of rope. His injured arm refused to rise in his defense, and it was the smack of his forehead striking a metal tie-down on the dock that eventually broke his fall.

NINE

Detective Shelton's last words to Stephanie before he rushed after Rick and Julian had been, "Stay in the car."

At first she obeyed his command, but that had been before she saw Julian's bullet rip into Rick's shoulder, before she watched Rick stagger from the impact, and before the *pop, pop, pop* sounds confirmed what her eyes were telling her brain.

Any instructions the detective had given her disappeared the moment she knew Rick was hurt. Her hands flung open the door handle and she was already running when Julian's body toppled into the water. She watched Rick trip and fall, his forehead bouncing off something on the dock, and then he rolled over and remained completely still.

She found a trail of blood beginning where Rick had first taken the bullet and leading to where he had eventually fallen. Stephanie backpedaled a few steps. What would she see when she got to him? Was she prepared for the worst? Detective Shelton and another dark-haired officer were kneeling next to Rick. The rest of the officers had spread out, continuing the search.

Rick still wasn't moving. Stephanie forced herself back into a run. She needed to see with her own eyes that Rick was only injured. He couldn't be dead. She skidded to a stop next to Rick's motionless body, skinning her knees in the process.

"Is he okay?" she asked, her voice shrill.

"He's alive," the detective said. "I've got to go after Hale. You two stay with him. Paramedics are on their way."

Stephanie wanted to beg the detective not to leave them, but he had already run off the docks yelling into his cell phone. Rick would want Detective Shelton to go after Hale, but Stephanie was scared.

Laying trembling fingers on Rick's neck, she checked his pulse and leaned her cheek down to his mouth to see if he was still breathing. The thump of his pulse was strong under her fingers, and his breath warmed her cheek. Her head flopped back and she breathed a prayer of gratitude.

"He's breathing," she told the young cop on the other side of Rick.

"Yes, but we need to stop the bleeding," he said.

Her eyes took in all of the blood coming from Rick's shoulder and forehead. The smell of it made her stomach roll in waves that crested at the top of her throat. She fought against the wooziness. She couldn't pass out. Rick needed her. But she had never had much of a stomach for seeing other people's blood, and this was the most blood she had seen in her whole life.

Stephanie breathed in through her nose, counting to three with each inhale, then exhaling through her mouth, calming the nausea the best that she could. They had to stop the bleeding, but which wound was the most important to treat first? The forehead was bleeding the heaviest, but didn't all head wounds bleed profusely, even if they were minor? She had had some first-aid training in preparation for her mission trips, but gunshot wounds were way outside of her league.

Detective Shelton said the paramedics were coming; she could hear the sirens, but she didn't think Rick could wait that long for them to get to him.

The officer ripped a section off the bottom of Rick's T-shirt, revealing Rick's muscular stomach, as well as multiple jagged scars covering his abdomen and chest.

Stephanie sucked in a deep breath, stunned at the sight of all of those scars. She didn't want to imagine the pain they represented. She remembered feeling similar scars on Axle when she had petted him in the hotel. Intense admiration and compassion filled her for the unconscious man on the ground in front of her.

What kind of battle were you two in to get those?

"Here, use this and put gentle pressure on his forehead," the officer said, handing her part of Rick's shirt. "I'll take a look at his shoulder."

She gently applied the cloth to Rick's bleeding head. She watched as the officer examined Rick's shoulder. She could see where the bullet had entered and exited his shoulder. Not having the bullet still in there had to be a good thing, wasn't it?

At the sound of the paramedics' running steps, Stephanie rolled back onto her heels, relieved. The closer they got, the more the dock swayed under her. She popped up and got out of the way, allowing the professionals to take over.

"How is he?" a deep voice asked from behind her. She spun and found that Detective Shelton had returned.

"I don't know," she answered in a voice barely above a whisper. "Did you catch Julian?"

"No sign of him. Every officer in the city is looking. We have helicopters in the air and a dive team prepping. I'm hoping Rick got him and we will find him on the bottom of the lake."

Please let them catch him. Let this nightmare end.

It probably wasn't any of her business, but her curiosity couldn't be contained. "Do you know where Rick got those scars on his stomach?" she asked the detective.

"Ah, those. Those came from being in the wrong place at the wrong time and running into a nut job with a knife. You'll have to ask Rick about that story when he wakes up."

Rick moaned, startling Stephanie. Was he waking up?

"Come on," Shelton said. "We'll meet the ambulance at the hospital." The detective sighed deeply and hung his head. "And I can guarantee that Rick is not going to be happy when he wakes up. He's already done enough time in that place."

"Officer Powell. Wake up, please."

Rick opened his eyes to a woman hovering over him. She was far too old for the hot-pink streak in her hair, and her raspy smoker's voice was far too chipper for 4:00 a.m. He was sick of her interrupting his sleep.

He squinted at the far wall. Under "Your Nurse's Name Is:" she had printed "Yvonne" in big slanted letters with a green dry-erase marker.

"And how are we feeling?" Yvonne asked as she checked his vitals. It was the same question she had just asked him an hour ago.

"Peachy," he mumbled. The whiteboard said Yvonne's shift ended at 7:00 a.m. Not soon enough for his liking. *I'd be better if you people would quit waking me up.*

Because of the concussion, the nurses had been waking him every hour to make sure he was still alive. It was annoying. The pain meds dripping through his IV made him want to sleep, but every time he closed his eyes, Yvonne's singsong voice dragged him back awake again.

The gown they had him wearing felt like a dress. His mind was groggy and his head and shoulder throbbed. It was probably time to ask Yvonne for more pain meds, but Rick preferred to feel the pain over the fog and fatigue brought on by the narcotics. He was done being weak and needy.

He hated everything about this place. The familiar muted sounds and smells of a hospital floor in the middle of the night seeped in from the hallway like a bad dream. He heard the squeak of a nurse's shoe and the swishing sounds and beeps of the multitude of medical equipment. He smelled the lingering odor of antibacterial soap Yvonne put on before examining him.

After they released him last year, he had promised himself that he would never return to this place. Yet here he was lying in the same hospital. No matter how hard he fought to make it line up with his desires, life kept going its own way, forging its own path. It made him want to push harder.

Light from the hallway broke through the semidarkness of the room, spotlighting the recliner next to his bed where Stephanie had curled up and fallen asleep. It looked uncomfortable, but at least the nurses had given her a blanket and a pillow.

His memory of what had happened since Hale's bullet hit him was fuzzy, but of what he could remember, Stephanie had been present the whole time.

Allie didn't stay. Allie didn't even make it through one night with me. Apparently the last time he had been in the hospital, three hours of bedside vigil had been his former fiancée's limit.

The last real conversation he'd had with Allie

had been in a hospital room like this one. It was even possible that this was the actual room where that conversation had taken place. This could be the same bed he had been lying in when Allie started weeping and told him, "I can't do this anymore, Rick. I love you, but we both know I am not cut out to be a cop's wife."

The strain his job placed on their relationship had been building for a long time. There had been one too many night shifts, and one too many plans ruined when he was held over for mandatory overtime. Seeing him near death in a hospital bed had been her breaking point.

He saw again Allie's tearful face, heard again her apologies as she slipped off the engagement ring. She had left the ring beside his water cup before she walked out the door, leaving a gaping wound no doctor could stitch back up for him.

"Rick?" Stephanie's sleepy voice asked from the recliner. "Are you awake?"

Rick worked to bring his mind out of the past. Stephanie kicked off her blanket and padded in her socks to his bedside. "Do you need anything?"

He stared at the ceiling. "Nah, I'm fine. Just ready to get out of this place. You didn't have to stay."

"Where was I supposed to go?" Stephanie

sat on the edge of his bed. "You're my body-guard, remember?"

He released bitter air between his lips. "Some bodyguard."

"I'm still alive, aren't I?"

"No thanks to me." He turned his head on the pillow to look at her. "Thanks for sticking around, though."

She waved her hand out in front of her. "Look at these luxury accommodations. There's even an officer standing guard out there in the hall-way. Where could I be that's any better than this?"

He gave her a thin smile. "I'm thankful for the company, but I wish you didn't have to be so uncomfortable. Hospitals are no fun."

"What do you mean? Yvonne isn't enough fun for you?"

Rick snorted in response. "Oh, yeah. She is loads of fun."

Stephanie placed a soft hand on top of his. He soaked up the comfort from it. Everything about her seemed soft in the dim light. Soft curls, soft pink lips. And although he couldn't see it, he knew her heart was soft, too. He couldn't help noticing again how very different she was from Allie.

Even in high school, Allie was sophisti-cated and high-maintenance. Moving into her twenties, she had become more and more polished, with a coolness that was alluring. But sitting next to him on the edge of his hospital bed in the middle of the night, Stephanie was all lightness and ease. The warmth radiating from the inside out was so comfortable and inviting.

He really did appreciate her company, although *appreciate* felt like the wrong word. It was more than that; he felt it much deeper. He turned his hand over and squeezed hers, thankful that she hadn't pulled it away.

She continued, "Seriously, don't worry about me being uncomfortable. I really don't mind." Her voice light and teasing, she said, "I'm not the one with a bullet wound and a busted-open forehead."

"What? This?" he asked, lifting the bandaged arm. "It's merely a flesh wound."

He almost wished the bullet wound was more serious so he could blame it for being stuck in the hospital again. The bullet had entered and exited his shoulder without too much damage. They probably would have released him already if that was all that ailed him. It was the stupid bump on the head that had made the doctor insist that he stay overnight for observation. Taking a bullet was so much more heroic than tripping over his own feet.

Stephanie squirmed a little. "Can I ask you a question? It's kind of personal."

He winced. "You saw the scars?"

"Yeah"

"Pretty ugly, huh?"

"More like badges of honor. I was pretty impressed, actually."

She glanced down at their hands clasped together, and said in a quieter voice, "I felt the scars on Axle's belly, too, and I have been wondering about it, but you don't have to talk about it if you don't want to." She tried to pull her hand away, but he grasped it tighter, unwilling to break the connection so soon.

Until now, he had not wanted to discuss that night. He had been too busy trying to recover, and he'd resented everyone wanting him to relive the nightmare. It had been important to put it all behind him and move on. But talking to Stephanie felt natural. He wanted her to know him.

"I was working a night shift, and I got an alarm call from the Industrial District. A security guard thought he saw suspicious activity going on at the warehouse across the street from his building." Rick's mind took him back. "I wasn't too concerned. We had been slammed with a string of false alarms at businesses all year long. While I waited for my backup, Axle and I searched the perimeter. I had no idea that we had actually stumbled onto a holding site for a human trafficking ring. Several women and girls were being held prisoner inside that building until they could be moved to some other location along the I-5 corridor. We must have spooked their guards when we showed up. One of them jumped us with a knife."

Stephanie's fingers squeezed his hand gently, encouraging him to keep going with the story. That night, Rick had been maybe fifteen feet back from rounding the building when a man flew around the corner at him wielding a knife. He had been trained to understand how fast and lethal a knife could be. He knew how within seconds fingers could be sliced off or tendons severed, or how within the span of those same seconds, a person could be lying on the ground with a knife sticking out of a vital organ. But no amount of training scenarios could have prepared him for the speed and intensity of the real thing.

Looking back, he was able to recall the man's face. In his dreams he still saw how those eyes were filled with both rage and fear simultaneously. But in the moments of the attack, Rick had had no time to observe. There had only been time to act. The scene replayed across his memory again now. He saw the flashes of movement in sync with his heartbeat, the glint of streetlight off the blade, slashing, slashing and then stabbing. He saw his gun rising, heard the bullets, as round after round fired from his gun. He saw his assailant crumple to the ground, dead. Rick had killed a man.

Rick closed his eyes, but kept talking. "I was finally able to fire my gun, but not before his knife had done a lot of damage to both me and Axle."

"Wow." Stephanie was quiet for a while. Then she said, "Those women owe you their freedom, Rick. It sounds like a story from a third-world country, but not here, not in America."

"It's more common here than anyone wants to admit."

"You're a hero," she said.

Rick shook his head, making him dizzy. "I'm no hero. I just stumbled onto that situation and barely made it back out alive."

She didn't say anything more, and Rick didn't feel the need to talk more, either. He had avoided talking about that night for so long, it surprised him how easily it had spilled out of him and how good it felt to tell her.

Rick wasn't sure how much time passed before he remembered that he was holding Stephanie's hand again. He did not want to let go of her, but the very room they were sitting in reminded him of the way he had failed Allie. He couldn't want this. Yes, Stephanie was a very different woman from Allie, but she was still a woman who deserved better than what he would be able to offer her. What she needed from him was to help her stay safe, not to be confused by his developing feelings for her. He let go, hating how empty his hand felt after he did.

She cleared her throat and stood up. "You better go back to sleep while you can," she said, a teasing tone returning to her voice. "It won't be long before you get another visit from your friend Yvonne."

"Okay," he said, fatigue pulling him under fast. "But be ready to go early. If you aren't firing me as your bodyguard, I've got a new plan."

TEN

Detective Shelton leaned against the doorjamb of Rick's hospital room. He sighed and made an announcement: "No sign of Hale, in or out of the water."

Stephanie's head dropped. She had heard the news from another officer in the ER waiting room, but she hadn't had the courage to tell Rick last night. She had been holding out hope for Julian's being caught overnight. Her eyes flew to Rick to see his reaction. He struggled to sit up in his bed, worrying her that he would reopen his stitches. She ran to his side to help him, but he waved her off. His anger was palpable.

"How could that happen?" Rick demanded. "We had him in the water."

The detective's shoulders slumped. "We searched all day and through the night. They brought the dogs. Divers looked for his body in the water. We had helicopters in the air. All manpower not tied up in the bombing investigation at the hotel scoured the area. Somehow he pulled another disappearing act on us. I'm thinking he must have slipped out of the water and into the downtown crowd while we were still on the dock. With all that construction happening, I'm guessing he was gone before we even got the search truly off the ground."

Rick punched the bed with his good hand. Even though it was Stephanie's life being threatened, Julian's capture was just as important to these two men as it was to her. Having these driven men on her side made her feel somehow safer, even if Julian Hale was still out there somewhere. These two would not stop until she was safe again. Actually they wouldn't stop until all of Seattle was safe from him again.

"There was some good news from yesterday, though," Detective Shelton said.

"Really? I'm definitely ready for some good news," Stephanie told him.

"Hale is taking risks he hasn't taken in the past. He is so desperate to prove that he is in control and holding the power, his pride is going to be his downfall. At some point he is going to trip up, and we are going to be there to get him when he does."

"I hope you're right," Rick said. "But if Hale

is still loose, then Stephanie and I need to get out of here, the sooner the better." He swung his legs over the edge of the bed. All the color drained from his face and he dropped his head into his hand.

"Dizzy?" Stephanie asked, but this time she held herself back, not wanting to annoy him again by being too helpful.

"I'm fine," Rick said, but he kept his head on his hand. "Or at least I will be," he conceded.

The doctor had ordered a twenty-four-hour watch on his concussion. It was 7:00 a.m., six hours short of the twenty-four-hour mark. Stephanie tried to reason with Rick. "But why the hurry? We're safe here, aren't we?"

Rick lifted his head off his hand and squinted at her as if she had a third eye. "Safe? Like we were in the hotel?" He put his head back in his hand. "Do you want to wait around for Hale to deliver another present for you? Maybe I'll call down and order breakfast and see what he has next on the menu."

"All right, I get it." He didn't have to be such a jerk about it. Where had the softness she had seen in him the night before gone? He was being so cold to her this morning. "I'm just worried about you. You don't seem ready to go anywhere."

"If you want to worry about something, worry

about the kind of damage Julian Hale could do here if we stay," Rick told her.

Imagining another bomb going off, this time in the hospital full of fragile people, was enough to make Stephanie swallow her other retorts. They might be safer in here, but the other patients wouldn't be safe if they stayed. She and Rick were like Jonah on the ship during the storm when he fled from Nineveh—throw them out and the hospital would be a safe haven again. If Rick was physically capable of leaving, they really did need to get far away.

"Where do we go from here?" she asked. "Last night you said you had a new plan."

"As soon as I can break out of here," Rick said, looking anxious to make that happen soon, "I am taking you camping."

"Camping?" she asked, but he wouldn't elaborate.

Stephanie signaled and then double-checked over her shoulder before changing lanes. She wiped her sweaty palms on her jeans one at a time. It had been a long time since she had driven any vehicle in the city traffic, let alone one as big as Rick's pickup. Even with a dog in the backseat, it smelled masculine and clean and *new*.

Rick's head rested against the passenger seat

with his eyes closed. She was glad he couldn't critique her driving, but she still worried she would mess up and do something to damage his truck. *Watch me crash a police officer's $30,000 truck.*

She looked over at Rick, hating how pale he looked. During the hospital discharge process, they had handed him painkillers and a prescription for more as needed, but so far he had refused to take any of them, claiming he wanted to stay sharp. From her perspective, he didn't look alert; he only looked miserable. She wished she knew how to help, but he'd probably be too stubborn to accept her help, anyway, even if she did know what to do.

He still hadn't explained the new plan to her, but she didn't want to bother him to ask about it. Before they left the hospital, Detective Shelton had brought Rick a change of clothes, given him his gun and cell phone, and dropped off Axle along with Rick's truck. Nobody had told Stephanie anything except to drive the truck around to the entrance. She had pulled through the circular driveway and found Rick with a police escort and a volunteer who had wheeled him out in a wheelchair. He hadn't opened his eyes since he had climbed into the cab of the truck. All he had said to her was, "Start driving north."

She had fought the urge to salute him with a "Yes, sir." Why wouldn't he just tell her where they were going?

She glanced sideways again. She didn't think he was actually sleeping. *He's probably awake and just doesn't want to see it happen when I total his truck.*

A red Mazda Miata chose that moment to zip in front of her without signaling, forcing her to stomp on the brake. "Nice blinker, dude," she hollered after him. The driver waved his apology as he whipped ahead of her and off the next exit.

"Relax," Rick said without opening his eyes, his face pinched with pain. That sudden stop couldn't have felt good.

"That's easy for you to say. I don't even know where I'm going."

Rick slowly sat up and moved the car seat back into an upright position. "We are going to my grandparents' cabin on the Skagit River. It's in the mountains off the North Cascades Highway about two hundred miles from here. It's the most remote place I know to go. I'm hoping it's remote enough to finally shake Hale off our trail."

"You never know with Julian, though, do you?" she said. "But why didn't you tell me where we were going? Why all this secrecy?"

"Maybe I'm getting paranoid, but I'm sick of Hale popping up like a Whac-a-Mole everywhere we go. I figured the fewer people who knew our plans, the better."

"Including me?" She probably sounded snarky, but the lack of sleep was making her feel grumpy, and she didn't like being kept in the dark.

"Of course not. When could I have explained things to you without being overheard?"

"You should have found a way. I deserve to know what's going on." She blew a curl out of her eyes and stared ahead.

"Fair enough," he mumbled.

She signaled and changed lanes again, looking for the nearest exit for I-5 North. "Do you think he has someone telling him where we are?" she asked Rick.

"I don't know. I can't imagine anyone in the department feeding Hale information, but I still can't figure out how he's tracking us. Until I know how he's doing it, we have to be careful who we trust. That's why Shelton and I decided to decrease our security detail and to keep our plans quiet. I have two buddies from the department—Russ Miller and Jason King—who will meet us up at the cabin, but other than that there are only a select few in the loop."

Stephanie searched the traffic behind her in

the rearview mirror. All the cars and drivers looked like innocent, bored commuters to her. "How will I know if he's following us?"

"You won't be able to tell in the city. We'll stop in Marysville for food and supplies. The traffic will thin out after that and we'll be able to tell more." He leaned his head back and closed his eyes again. "Hopefully we'll catch a break for once."

Stephanie agreed. *And hopefully the nice Rick from last night will come back.*

After the stop for supplies and a run through the McDonald's drive-through window, Rick noticed that Stephanie's death grip on the wheel began to loosen. The farther north they drove, the more they both seemed to relax. He kept an eye on the traffic around and behind them, but he didn't see anything suspicious. It didn't mean Hale hadn't followed them again, but if he had, Rick couldn't see him.

He wasn't used to being a passenger, but the dizziness was still too strong for him to drive safely. The over-the-counter painkiller he had swallowed with his soda at lunch had taken the edge off his pain, though, and eventually he began enjoying the drive. As they started the slow climb up into the Cascade Mountains, the scenery became less urban and more rustic and nostalgic by the minute. It was the background of so many of his childhood memories.

"The highway reopened only a few weeks ago, so the road might be a little rough," he told Stephanie. "They always close it for the winter."

Stately evergreens lined the highway, and giant mountains still wearing their winter white loomed all around them. "Ever been across this pass before?" he asked Stephanie.

"No," Stephanie answered. "It's gorgeous."

Rick agreed. "They call these the American Alps."

She leaned forward and peered through the windshield. "I grew up in Eastern Washington, but we always took Stevens or Snoqualmie Pass to get to Seattle. Those passes have pretty views, but this…this is…wow."

Rick smiled. It was fun seeing it all anew through Stephanie's eyes. She was having a hard time keeping her eye on the road as she gawked at the passing vistas.

"Wow," she said again.

"I spent a lot of time up here as a kid fishing with my grandpa Powell," Rick said, gazing at the Skagit River running along the highway. The river surged strong and high, bloated with spring melt. It would be another month before they opened the season for chinook. Rick longed to have a fly rod in his hands.

"I wish it was good fishing right now," he told her. "Actually, fall is my favorite time of year to fish up here, though. You should see how beautiful it is when the trees are on fire with color."

Rick almost added, *I'll have to bring you up here again then and teach you how to fish,* but he remembered that his protection duty would be over long before the leaves turned. Stephanie wouldn't be a part of his life by then. Besides, who knew if she would even be interested in fishing?

"I grew up in a house full of girls. I've never even touched a fishing pole," she admitted. "It sounds fun."

"It is fun," Rick said. "But it's more than that for me. More like an art, or an obsession. Some people paint, I guess I fish."

"I thought fishing was a summer sport," she said.

"No." Rick chuckled. "If I try hard enough, I can find somewhere to fish year round. Coho run in the fall, and on odd years, we get a good humpy run then, too."

Rick sighed, soaking up the scenery. It had been too long since he'd gotten away from the city. He used to fish every chance he got, but he had been too preoccupied with recovery and rehab to make the drive up here. Prior to his injury, he had wanted to come, but Allie hated leaving civilization behind. How long *had* it been since he'd had a fishing pole in his hands?

Axle whimpered from the backseat. The dog stared longingly out the back windows, probably imagining a romp through the woods. "Not much longer now, buddy, and you can get out and run," Rick assured him.

About an hour later, Rick directed Stephanie to turn off the main highway, and they began weaving along the opposite banks of the meandering Skagit River until they arrived at the old wooden Powell Family sign. His nana had hand-painted it herself to mark the top of their private lane.

Stephanie giggled as the truck bumped along the rutted path. "Just try to find us all the way out here, Julian Hale."

Rick sat up straight and leaned forward, eager to spot the cabin site. As the trees thinned and the A-frame cabin with its wraparound porch and sloped green metal roof greeted his hungry eyes, he felt all of the weariness and heartache he had been carrying around with him throughout the past year begin to evaporate. He flopped back against the car seat, his lips curling up at the corners.

He was home.

ELEVEN

Tuesday Night

Rick's eyelashes fluttered as he fought to clear his vision and to wake up his mind. Moonlight slipped through the slats of the venetian blinds, projecting white stripes across his nana's patchwork quilt. He remembered arriving at the cabin and helping Stephanie unload the supplies. Then his coworkers Russ Miller and Jason King had shown up to help with security. Rick had known he could trust them to take over, so he'd crawled into this bed and crashed. He had no idea how much time had passed since then. He smacked his dry tongue against the roof of his mouth. He needed water. His stomach rumbled. And food.

Rick squinted at the red block numbers of the alarm clock. It read 9:00 p.m. His hand slapped around on the nightstand until his fingers found his cell phone. He held it above his head, grimacing away from the bright glare in the dark room.

He sat straight up. The time on the alarm clock was correct, but the date on the phone said he had slept longer than a few hours. He had slept all of the night before and through the following day. He hopped out of bed and jogged down the hallway to the living room in search of Stephanie and Axle.

He found Stephanie wrapped in a quilt, fast asleep, with Axle cuddled up next to her on the couch. A warm glow from the fireplace enhanced the cozy scene. Rick sighed, his concern melting away. It didn't look as if they had missed him too much. He may have failed as a bodyguard, but they both appeared to have survived just fine without him.

In the kitchen, he found Miller and apologized for sleeping through his guard duty shifts. Miller assured him that he and King had been fine.

"It's been uneventful," he said, stifling a yawn. Rick still felt the guilt of shirking his duty. King had driven up a fifth wheel trailer for the two men to stay in, but he doubted they had gotten much downtime yet with Rick sleeping through his turn standing watch. From the look of boredom and fatigue on Miller's face, Rick could see the man was ready to be off duty.

"I need a quick shower and then I can take over," Rick said. "I've had enough sleep to carry me through the night shift and then some."

After showering and grabbing the two-way radio from Miller, Rick meandered back into the living room feeling refreshed. His sense of time was still disoriented, but the dizziness and pain from the concussion and the wound on his shoulder had lifted considerably. It felt good to be up and out of bed.

He sat, balancing on the back edge of the couch, and peered down at Stephanie. Her long blond eyelashes rested on her cheeks in peaceful sleep. She seemed to fit here in this simpler environment more than she did in the busy city. There was a rare sweetness to her that he liked. A desire to protect her beat inside him stronger than ever. Miller and King were good guys and great cops. He had left her in capable hands, but he didn't want her to be anyone else's responsibility.

When had keeping her safe shifted from being a favor for Terrell to being something he wanted to do for himself? Maybe it had happened when he heard her yelling for him in the hotel stairway after the bomb, or maybe it was when she held his hand and stayed with him in the hospital. All he knew was he had to do a better job of watching out for her now that he was awake and somewhat recovered.

He tucked a few stray curls behind one of her ears to get a clearer view of her face. She had such a fresh beauty. Her sun-kissed skin was flawless but for the few freckles that crossed her nose. At his touch, Stephanie turned her face into his hand. He cupped her cheek while his thumb gently ran across her eyebrow. He hadn't noticed before that her right eyebrow arched a bit higher than her left one, giving her a look of constant curiosity. Why would anyone want to hurt her?

"Wake up, sleeping beauty," he whispered.

He absentmindedly played with the piping along the edge of the couch as he fought his desire to kiss her. He leaned down, his lips hovering above her face. He gently kissed the tip of her nose and popped back up to standing. What was he doing? Being in the cabin, a place of so many warm and secure memories, was messing with his brain and making him too relaxed.

There were several days left in the week he had promised Terrell. He didn't want to spend those days constantly fighting the temptation to kiss Stephanie. If he was going to succeed in keeping her safe, he needed to be able to focus. He walked to the fireplace, pretending to warm his hands. Anything to distract him from her lips.

Stephanie stretched and said in a sleepy voice, "You're awake." She kicked off the quilt and joined him in front of the fire. Putting her hand on his elbow, she asked, "Feeling better?"

He jumped a little at her touch. Her face had a look of such sincere concern, he had to fight himself even more. "Much better, but I didn't mean to abandon you like that."

She shrugged her right shoulder. "It wasn't a big deal. Your friends kept us safe. I was glad Julian left us alone long enough for you to get the rest you needed. Maybe we've finally found a good hiding place."

Axle slid off the couch into a full body stretch on the floor, followed by a noisy yawn, and then weaseled his way between the two of them. "Axle and I have been fine, haven't we?" Stephanie said as she petted the top of Axle's head. When she stopped, Axle bumped her hand with his head, insisting that she keep up the petting. Stephanie obliged him, and asked Rick, "What breed is Axle?"

"He's a Belgian Malinois." Talking about Axle always made him proud. "Malies are quick and smart. They make great police dogs." He reached down to pet Axle, and as he did his fingers brushed against Stephanie's hand on Axle's back. Only their pinkies touched, but Rick could feel the contact down into his core. For a few beats, neither of them moved their hand away. The corners of Stephanie's mouth tipped up into a small, demure smile.

Rick was the first to move. He shoved his hands into his pockets, thankful that Axle acted as a barrier between him and Stephanie. Rocking back on his heels, Rick said. "I hope His Royal Highness hasn't been too demanding of you while I was out of it. He's looking a little spoiled to me."

Stephanie continued massaging Axle's withers. "Nah. He's been a good boy. We've had fun. I called my school and checked in with my principal, and then I found the bookshelf." She lifted up the half-read novel she held in her other hand. "I feel like I'm on a vacation."

Warmth spread throughout him. He loved this place. It felt good to have someone else to share it with, someone who appreciated it and wasn't itching to get back to the city. He pointed at the crackling fire. "Did you do that?"

She looked sheepish. "It got chilly, and I found the firewood." Her right eyebrow arched even higher. "Was that okay?"

Rick turned his back to the fire's warmth. "It's great. I'm impressed."

She rewarded his compliment with a full

smile that reached her eyes and made them dance in the firelight. The dim glow from the fireplace softened her already-beautiful features, the orange hues reflecting in her blue eyes and lighting up the red highlights in her hair. Rick stepped around Axle, and moved so close to her that only inches separated them. He breathed in her faint perfume. He was losing his resolve.

The same rebellious curls he had tucked behind her ear when she was sleeping had fallen forward again. He reached out for them, winding the silky strands around his finger. His breathing slowed, deepening further when Stephanie didn't pull away. She looked up at him, her mouth so close, all it would take was a decision and his lips would find hers.

He let go of her hair. "I think we better say good-night before I forget my job," he whispered and then cleared his throat.

Stephanie placed her open palm on his chest. "Rick, I…"

"Trust me, I want to kiss you," he interrupted her, backing away. "But it's complicated."

She dropped her hand and blinked, the moment broken for both of them as reality came rushing in like cold air. "Yeah, *complicated* is a good word for me, too."

She turned and walked toward the stairs that

led up to the room she was using, leaving him alone by the fireplace. He planted his feet. He wanted to follow her, to pull her back into his arms and kiss her the way his brain was screaming for him to do, but it was Stephanie who returned to him. She stood so close, he could see himself reflected back in her eyes. Stephanie took both of his hands in hers. "Rick?"

He groaned inwardly. Her eyes were so blue.

"Yeah?" He ran his thumbs over the backs of her hands.

"Thank you. For everything. I don't know what I would have done."

"It's okay."

"No. I've been thinking about it all so much while you were sleeping. I don't know how I'm ever going to repay you for all of this. I am so grateful to be alive and safe and in this place. Thank you." The sheen of grateful tears over her eyes made them look like tiny tide pools.

He weaved his fingers into her hair and pulled her close enough to kiss her forehead. Then he turned her by the shoulders away from him. "Now go to bed. You're killing me. You have no idea how beautiful you look in this light."

She giggled. "Me? You should get a look at yourself."

She began climbing the stairs, but before

she reached the top, Rick made a decision and stopped her. "Stephanie?"

"Yes?" Her now-familiar arched eyebrow rose higher like an endearing question mark.

"Make sure you get lots of rest." He grinned. "I think you've been cooped up long enough. Tomorrow you are going to learn how to shoot a gun."

TWELVE

Wednesday

"Ready to make some stuff blow up?" Rick teased her.

No. Her insides wobbled like Jell-O. Stephanie had never touched a gun. Growing up on the rural eastern side of Washington State, she had gone to school with plenty of boys—and some girls, too—who drove trucks with gun racks. Many of them took two weeks off school every November to hunt elk. But living with just her sister and her mom, the only guns Stephanie had ever seen up close were on TV.

Rick unlocked his grandfather's oak gun cabinet and handed her a rifle. In her hands, it was lighter than it looked, but still cumbersome. She shifted it around, trying to figure out the right way to hold it.

"Whoa!" Rick ducked. Laughing, he said, "Give me that thing."

Her face flushed. This was a very bad idea. She had no clue what she was doing holding a gun. She couldn't hand it back to him fast enough.

"Rule number one," he said. "The gun is always loaded."

Her eyes widened. "Is it loaded right now?" She licked her lips, her mouth suddenly very dry. The way she had been swinging that gun around, she could have fired it in the cabin by accident.

"Whether it is or isn't loaded doesn't matter. You treat it as if the gun is always loaded, and you don't point it at anything, or *anyone*, that you don't intend to shoot." He tried to put it back in her hands, but she shook her head. He wouldn't take no for an answer, though, pushing it back into her grip. "The safety is on, and just to make you feel better, it is not loaded at the moment."

She scrambled for more excuses to postpone the shooting lesson. "But is it safe for me to be outside?"

"We are so remote up here and we haven't heard from Julian in two days—we'll be fine. We're well hidden, but to be on the safe side, Miller just did a sweep of the area where I'm taking you, and he and King are going to patrol the road. We're going to be just fine."

Axle pushed past them and out the cabin door. He flew off the porch in hot pursuit of a chipmunk. Rick and Stephanie followed him into the sunshine. A sharp bite in the air and the visible puffs of their breath showed that winter was still clinging on at this elevation, but on this bright morning, spring popped up everywhere. Patches of green peeked through the residual snow and although it was chilly, bright sunshine claimed the blue sky, proclaiming hope. They couldn't have asked for a prettier day to spend outside. It was the perfect cure for the cabin fever she had been feeling. Stephanie inhaled the crisp air through her nose, and exhaled a prayer. *Thank You that I'm alive to see this beauty.*

She jogged to catch up with Rick, careful to point the gun she carried down and away as he had instructed her. Axle reveled in his freedom, bolting ahead of them, chasing more chipmunks and barking at birds. Rick carried a blanket, the ammunition they would need, two pistols and a picnic lunch they had packed.

If it weren't for the scary guns and bullets part, Stephanie might enjoy the romance of this whole excursion. Flashbacks of the night before and the almost-kiss in front of the fireplace made her blush. It was a good thing Rick had been thinking logically, because she sure hadn't been, and given another chance she wasn't sure she would have resisted.

The river's edge was covered with loose rock. It was peaceful and remote, but not quiet. They had to raise their voices to hear each other over the roar of the bulging river as it carried down snowmelt. The highway ran high above the opposite bank. It was pretty far away, but the sounds of semi trucks and cars rounding the corner echoed off the cliffs near them, making it feel closer. It was the same highway she and Rick had driven only two days ago to get to the cabin. It had been such a peaceful two days it had almost slipped her mind why they were there, forgetting for a bit that her life was still in danger and this was not a vacation.

"There's a cut bank up here that will be perfect for setting up the targets," Rick called back to her. The little-boy grin on his face made her happy. "It's the same place I learned to shoot a gun." There was a skip in Rick's step she hadn't seen before. How fun would it have been to grow up coming to a place like this? It was kid paradise.

They stepped high over a sun-bleached log before Rick stopped and set down the cooler. He spread out the blanket, then knelt down to line up the boxes of ammo and the two pistols. He reached up for her rifle. Stephanie handed it to him, trying to appear brave. Had she fooled him or could he read her thoughts of *scared, scared, scared*?

He squinted up at her. "Lunch or lessons first?"

Stephanie chewed her bottom lip. "Better do the lessons first." Her stomach ached from nerves, and her throat was so dry she couldn't swallow. She should have thought to grab a water bottle from the cabin before they left. *I don't want to do this.*

Rick lined the targets up against a sheer cliff the rushing water had worn away over the years. He talked while he worked. "So, when I was in your apartment, I noticed a lot of African decor. Have you been to Africa?" She knew he was trying small talk in order to ease her nerves. So she hadn't hidden her fear very well after all. His attempts to calm her were sweet.

"I've been to Liberia several times, actually." Stephanie was surprised by the emotion that hit her thinking about her love for the country. "My younger sister and her husband are missionaries there, and my plan is to join them as soon as I can afford it."

"Really?" He turned away from the targets and walked back to the blanket. He seemed genuinely taken aback; then again, how many girls could he possibly know who were planning to run off to West Africa? *Probably just one.*

"Will you teach there?" he asked.

She shrugged her shoulders. "I'm not sure. It's all so unsettled. My dream is to work with orphans, but I'm not exactly sure how to finance it all yet." Talking about Liberia reminded her that running from Julian wasn't the only part of her life in limbo. "To be honest, it's kind of driving me crazy," she admitted. "I keep waiting for the big neon sign, you know? The one that says God's Will Is This Way."

She hung her head. "I only know I need to do something more meaningful than what I'm doing now. I want to make God happy, but He isn't talking yet and all of the doors are still shut."

Rick was quiet for a moment. She wished she could read his thoughts. "I'm sure your students would say your job is pretty meaningful," he said. "My fifth-grade teacher got me through my parents' divorce." Then he dropped the subject and picked up one of the handguns off the blanket. "Well, Miss Future Missionary, are you ready to learn how to shoot this thing?"

"Ready," she lied.

"I know you aren't thrilled about this, but once you get familiar with shooting it won't seem so scary. After you hit a few targets, you might even start to have fun." He turned the gun over in his hand. "This .45 will be a good one to start with."

Stephanie eyeballed the gun in his hand as if it were another bomb about to explode. "Tell me again why I need to do this? Even if I know how to shoot it, that doesn't mean I could ever actually shoot someone."

"Even someone bent on killing you or threatening someone you love?"

"I don't know. It isn't a moral dilemma I've wrestled much with before now." She didn't like the way that question made her squirm.

"What if Julian was about to harm Joash or Haddie?"

She didn't answer so he went on. "I keep thinking about the other night at the Watkinses' place. I keep seeing the kids sliding around the kitchen in their socks and how excited they were about eating their dessert in the living room." Rick's forehead scrunched up with emotion. Stephanie replayed the scene in her own mind as he spoke, her stomach twisting.

Rick stared at the gun in his hands. "Julian Hale lit a house on fire that he knew had innocent women and kids inside…" Rick looked into her eyes and said, "This guy is serious, Stephanie." He held up the gun in his hand. "It makes me sick thinking that he might hurt you. I need to know you can defend yourself."

When she nodded, he began, "Okay, lesson number one review... The gun is always loaded..."

Her stomach was Jell-O again, and her hands felt unnaturally light. Rick taught her how to slap in the magazine and how to chamber the bullet, then the gun was all hers. His arms encircled her from behind, showing her how to hold the gun properly. "Remember." His mouth was so close she felt the air skim her ear as he spoke, but with the orange foam earplugs in, he had to shout for her to hear him. "Finger off the trigger until you are ready to shoot."

She held the pistol straight out in front of her. Rick's hands gripped her waist. "Relax. Bend your knees. Lean in to it." She tried to remember all of the instructions he had rattled off about the different stances, the breathing, squeezing versus pulling the trigger, not trying to anticipate the noise.

Rick pointed at the orange disks sitting in metal stands against the cut bank. They looked like the bottoms of flower pots. "Line up your sights on the target. Good." He leaned with her, talking her through the steps. "Okay. As soon as you're ready, go ahead." He let go of her and stepped away.

"Wait. I'm not ready."

"Once you blow up one of those targets you'll be hooked." He crossed his arms and waited for her to squeeze the trigger. *Squeeze, not pull.* She remembered that much. *Or was it the other way around?*

"Any day now, Stephanie," Rick teased. "It's nothing more than target practice. Bend your knees. Don't try to anticipate the—"

Bang. Bang. Bang. Bang. Bang.

All five of the targets exploded, one after the other, orange fragments flying through the air.

"Whoa!" Rick was flabbergasted. His hands flew to the top of his head. He hopped around in excitement. "I can't believe it. You hit every one of them."

Stephanie still held her arms up, frozen in place. Then suddenly she fell prone in the dirt and screamed, "Rick, get down."

He knelt beside her and asked, "Did you faint? That can happen…"

"Rick, get down!" She popped up and tackled him to the ground. She looked down into his confused face. "I never pulled the trigger."

Bullets peppered the ground, preventing him from standing. Rick pushed Stephanie off him and grabbed the gun she still clutched in her hand. The shots came from somewhere behind them, on the other side of the river.

Rick rolled and fired, searching for cover. They were too exposed by the river, but the tree line was too far to run without getting shot. He spotted the log they had climbed over earlier. It was small, but some cover was better than none. "Follow me," he shouted to her. Grabbing her hand, they bolted for the log.

Only a few paces away, the ground in front of the log exploded with rapid bullets splaying rocks, knocking them to the ground for the second time. Rick landed on top of Stephanie, shielding her body from the raining lead. "You're okay, Steph. Hang on," he shouted into her ear.

Lord, save us. Rick was praying for the first time in too long. It was true, the old saying about remembering God in foxholes. His prayer life had been nonexistent lately. *I've been trying to fix this whole mess on my own, trying to keep Stephanie and everyone else safe in my own strength.* A bullet hit to his left, spraying gravel into his eyes. Stephanie coughed underneath him.

You could hit us if you wanted to. Where are you, Hale?

Cliffs and plateaus surrounded the river on

both sides, providing a number of perfect hiding spots for a sniper. The highway traffic masked the noise, and the shooter had the perfect vantage point to see their defenseless position below. They were sitting ducks. With the right scope and a regular hunting rifle, even an average shot could pick them off from three to four hundred yards away. It had to be Julian Hale. Wherever he was hiding, it was far enough to remain unseen, but close enough to completely destroy their targets with perfect aim.

Stephanie whimpered at each *ping* of a bullet. Rick winced, expecting pain.

Rick returned fire, shooting blind. His bullets sprayed rocks less than one hundred yards away. He couldn't risk hitting a car on the highway. As he continued firing and praying for their safety, the bullets hit close but never struck them.

"He's playing games with us again," he yelled, hoping to somehow reassure Stephanie.

Then as quickly as they had begun falling, the bullets completely stopped. Rick counted ten seconds. Did he dare move? His body weight was surely crushing Stephanie underneath him.

Rick army-crawled to the blanket and grabbed the rifle, then crawled back to where Stephanie lay on the ground. He pulled the two-way radio off his belt and called for help.

Miller's voice crackled. "We're on the highway. We'll find him."

No more shots fired.

"Leave everything and run for the trees," Rick told Stephanie. "Stay low and get inside the cabin.

"I'm right behind you all the way, okay? I'll be firing the gun to cover us. You do not stop. No matter what you think is happening behind you, you do not stop until you are safe inside. Understand?"

Stephanie's pupils dominated her irises, but she scrambled up and began to run. Rick moved to follow after her, but in his peripheral vision he spotted movement. A blur of brown fur burst from the tree line farther down the river.

"Axle, *bleib*! *Bleib!*" Rick screamed the command for *stay* over and over and over again, but the dog either couldn't hear him or simply refused to obey.

Lord, help, Stephanie prayed. She couldn't find any other words to string together. That would have to be enough.

Was this what war felt like? Feeling the futility of the situation, knowing the enemy was stronger than you? Waiting to be shot, wondering if each breath was the last before a bullet sliced through you?

When I'm shot, what will it feel like?

Rick had shoved her forward, shouting instructions at her, but her confused mind had jumbled them. *Run. To the cabin. Don't look back. Don't stop.*

"Go! Go! Go!"

The running felt surreal, as though she were moving through the landscape of a vaguely familiar nightmare. Stephanie didn't think, only ran. She remembered the foam earplugs were still in place. She popped them out and dropped them to the ground. She heard Rick's gun firing behind her, she heard him screaming something, but she did not stop.

Each step and heartbeat brought a question. Step. *Am I alive?* Beat. *Is Rick behind me?* Step. *How much farther?* Step. *Where is Axle?* She reached the tree line and the path toward the cabin. She stopped. *Wait, where is Axle?*

Stephanie spun around, searching before she even knew what she was looking to find. Her eyes locked on Rick crouched behind the log for cover. Why wasn't he following her? He promised he would be right behind her.

The desperation in the commands Rick screamed paralyzed her. A flash of brown drew her eye farther down the river's bank. Axle sprinted toward Rick, the dog's athleticism and heroic heart on display leaving her breathless. His determination to ignore Rick's commands and to protect his master sent her to her knees. She heard the shots firing again, hating how helpless she was to stop what was about to happen. Axle flew at Rick, knocking him to the ground. She covered her ears, unable to accept that Axle had been shot, unable to stand the raw agony she heard in the dog's wails of pain.

THIRTEEN

The bullets were silent again, leaving only Axle's cries to compete with the river's roar. Each of the dog's painful yelps entered Rick's heart like a knife.

"Oh, buddy. I'm so sorry." Rick's hands shook as they hovered over Axle's writhing body. He was afraid to touch, but he needed to search for the wound. He gently worked through the fur, looking for where the bullet entered. He found a small hole in the back of his upper right shoulder and a larger exit wound on his front shoulder. He must have taken the bullet as he dived through the air for Rick.

"Hang in there, partner. You're going to be okay." Rick continued to croon words of comfort as he worked, trying to keep Axle still.

"You have to be okay." Tears welled, threatening to fall. Not much could make Rick cry. When he was a kid, if his dad or his grandfathers ever caught him crying, they would insist he knock it off and act like a man. Grandpa Powell would smack Rick on the arm and tell him to cowboy up. The last time he had cried was during his parents' divorce, in private, sitting inside his bedroom closet where no one could witness it. He hadn't even allowed himself to cry over Allie's leaving him.

With Axle quivering in pain before him, he was finding it difficult to cowboy up this time, but Axle needed him to be strong and to think clearly without letting the emotion take over. Rick willed away the tears. He would not lose Axle. He wouldn't even allow himself to think it. They hadn't battled this hard to survive these past months to have it end like this.

"You coward!" Rick screamed across the river in the direction he thought Hale was hiding, but his accusation echoed back to his own ears. Hale probably couldn't hear him. Was he even still up there? The gutless cur had probably already run away.

Hale's rifle remained silent, tempting Rick to make a run for it himself. He needed to get Axle to the truck and go for help, but what if moving Axle hurt him more? It was a risk he was going to have to take. But before Rick could scoop the dog into his arms, Stephanie stepped out from the tree line and started running toward him.

She was supposed to be in the cabin and safe by now. "What are you doing? Go back," he hollered at her.

Ignoring him, she kept running, using a large flat piece of scrap metal as a shield.

He tried to wave her off, his voice hoarse from all of the yelling he had done. "Get back in the cabin. Are you insane?"

She slid to the ground next to them, spitting up pebbles as she landed. Fury at the ridiculous stunt she had just pulled pumped through his veins. "What were you thinking? Now I've got two of you to get out of here safely."

"No, Rick, you don't understand. It's okay. I've figured something out." She dropped the scrap metal on to the ground. "I found this by the cabin. We can use it to carry Axle, to keep him still in case he has any broken bones."

He shook his head. "I told you no matter what was happening behind you, you were to get inside that cabin."

"I know what you said," she shouted. "But Axle needs help, and he wouldn't be hurt at all if it weren't for me. Besides, I've figured something out. When I was watching from the trail it occurred to me." She looked at him as though her words should make perfect sense. Well, they didn't make any sense at all to him.

"What are you talking about?"

"Don't you see?" She reached for him and gripped his upper arms. "I am Axle's best shield."

Rick's jaw dropped at her absurd claim. Shield? Rick pulled from her grip and pointed to the other side of the river. "That man up there with the gun? Remember him, Stephanie? He is shooting at us in order to kill you. Have you forgotten that?"

"You don't understand." She crawled away from Rick across the gravel toward the blanket. Dragging it back, she covered the metal with it and made a bed for Axle.

There was no question. She had lost it, snapped somehow under the stress, but he didn't have time to figure her out. He scooped Axle gently onto the makeshift gurney and wrapped the blanket tightly around the dog. He hoped its warmth would prevent Axle from going into shock. He didn't like that Stephanie had put herself in so much danger to get it down here, but he had to admit he was thankful for the way to transport the sixty-five-pound dog without causing further injury.

"I'll pick up the rear, you lead," he told her.

"Rick, you aren't listening to me." She flung her hands in the air in frustration. "Keep me between you and Julian at all times."

"I am not letting you turn suicidal on me, Stephanie."

She grabbed his arm, looking desperate to make him understand her. "Trust me, Rick. Shooting me from a distance is not what Julian has in mind for me. I'm figuring out the way he operates. He won't hesitate to shoot you or Axle to prove his power or to get to me, but he won't shoot me."

She bit her lip, and then she added in a voice so quiet he almost couldn't hear it above the river, "I think he has other plans for me."

Her crazy theory had some merit. Sniper fire was not Hale's style. He strangled his victims, preferring a more up close and brutal method. Rick had seen files that Stephanie hadn't. The photographs of the women Hale had murdered played like a slideshow across his mind.

Rick remembered how long it had taken for the bomb to detonate at the hotel. Hale had protected Stephanie then, preserving her for his future plans. The FBI profile had said he was motivated by a need for power and dominance. Stephanie might be right. This could be another display of strength so she wouldn't forget who was in control. Even if he was willing to shoot Axle and Rick, Hale probably wouldn't be satisfied with killing Stephanie from afar.

Finally he conceded, "All right. But move quickly and stay low."

Rick's foot pressed on the accelerator, his truck tires squealing around the corners on the steep mountain highway. With every curve, inertia pressed him hard against the driver's side door. He was pushing the speed as far as he dared. He didn't want to hurt Axle further with all of the bumps and sharp turns. Any faster and the next bend might send them soaring off a cliff.

Stephanie attempted to hold Axle still in the backseat with one hand and search Rick's cell phone for the nearest vet office with her other hand. She read out loud the directions to the closest one she could find.

"It's in Sedro-Woolley. Can we make it in time?"

"We have to make it in time," he told her, or was he telling God how it was going to be?

Rick heard tears in Stephanie's songlike words as she comforted Axle. "Shhh. It's okay. It's okay. Hang in there, Axle. Not long now and we will get you all fixed up, boy."

"Axle's a fighter," Rick told Stephanie. The reassurance was for his own benefit as much as it was for hers. "He'll make it."

When Rick was still in the hospital after the

stabbing, the city bigwigs had decided they couldn't justify the huge vet bills for the surgeries Axle required. They concluded Axle was too badly injured to ever recover and that the most humane thing was to put him down. Rick had protested, begging from his hospital bed that they do all that was necessary to save Axle's life and he would personally cover the bills. No matter what they all thought, he was Rick's partner, and even if Axle never walked or ran or even worked again, he was Rick's friend, and Rick had never regretted that decision. Axle had fought so hard and come back stronger than ever, proving everybody wrong.

Rick glanced over his shoulder to the backseat again. Axle was still, calmed by Stephanie's soothing voice, breathing deeply through the pain. "You're a fighter, buddy. Don't forget that," he commanded Axle. Rick knew in his gut that Axle would make it. He had to make it.

Rick thought back to the fancy ceremony he and Axle had attended after they'd recovered. They were both awarded the Medal of Valor. When the mayor handed Rick the box at the ceremony, he had felt like a hack accepting it. The intent of the award was to celebrate officers who go above and beyond the call of duty, showing great bravery or heroism without thought to their own safety in the face of extreme danger. Rick hadn't done anything exceptionally brave that night. He walked into a trap and almost got himself killed is what he had done. He had expected a reprimand or an internal affairs investigation, not a medal. He had felt ridiculous accepting the praise, and as soon as he got home that night he hid the box in his underwear drawer.

Not Axle. Rick had never seen Axle prouder. When the mayor slipped that medal over the dog's head, Axle's chest puffed out and he sat up as tall as he could possibly stretch himself. Later that evening when Rick tried to lift the ribbon off Axle's neck, Axle had growled at him and bared his teeth. It took two days before Rick could coax him into letting the medal go, and it was only after Rick showed him where the medal would be displayed.

You are a fighter, Axle. You're a hero, too. Axle had just saved Rick's life. The dog he loved had just taken a bullet to protect him. Rick's heart ached. He pushed the accelerator a smidge farther. He would risk flying off the highway. He had to get to that vet in time.

Stephanie flipped through a copy of *Horse&Rider* magazine she had picked up off the end table in the waiting room, but she wasn't reading or even seeing, only occupying her hands. Rick paced. He sat down. He jumped back up. He paced some more. It was an excruciating wait, and she wished she knew how to comfort him. Every time she opened her mouth to say something, the words she planned seemed so cliché that she clamped her mouth shut again.

The staff behind the reception counter looked a little shell-shocked by the sheer number of law enforcement officers coming in and out the door of their tiny clinic. Stephanie wanted to say, *Welcome to my life.*

Shelton and another detective had made an appearance, and the Skagit County sheriff had stopped by to interview them, leaving behind deputies to guard the clinic while others searched for Julian. They were the second local agency to show up. Stephanie appreciated their presence. If Julian could find them in the middle of a national forest, he could find them anywhere. She had learned her lesson. Never again would she let down her guard.

The rest of the cops who squeezed into the room were off-duty SPD officers, coworkers of Rick's who had driven north to support him when they heard about what had happened to Axle. Stephanie was beginning to understand what people meant when they talked about the law enforcement brotherhood. It was an amazing community.

She tossed the magazine down and replaced it with *Vets Life* instead. An adorable black-and-white pig smiled at her from the cover. She flipped, flipped, flipped the pages, not even reading a sentence, until she gave up and tossed the magazine on top of the other one.

Resting her head back against the wall, she closed her eyes. It was making her crazy that she couldn't *do* anything to help Rick or Axle other than sit here.

Stephanie knew nothing about dogs or gunshot wounds, but Axle had been in so much pain when she and Rick carried him in through these doors. She opened one eye and looked at Rick. The relationship he had with Axle was more than a typical pet and owner. As heartbreaking as it would be to lose a pet, for Rick, losing Axle was losing a comrade, a partner, someone who had faced death alongside him.

She stood up and stretched. For a moment she couldn't remember what day it was. Only Wednesday? How was that even possible?

She walked over to Rick, still unsure of what to say. He stopped pacing when she stood in front of him. She took one of his hands and squeezed it. "Rick. It's going to be okay."

His expression iced over, and he jerked his hand away from her. Then pacing started again. "There are no guarantees, Stephanie. Outside of your civilian fairy-tale world, life usually isn't okay."

She didn't want to feel the anger burning in her. She wanted to be understanding, but all she could think of was *don't take this out on me*. Her nostrils flared as she breathed for composure. "You don't think I've seen my fair share of life? I'll skip the sob story about my dad abandoning us when I was only three years old, and the one about my mom checking out, counting on me to be the parent. I've been to *Africa*, Rick. I've seen life."

He looked at her with bloodshot eyes and a forlorn expression that melted away her anger. She stepped forward and embraced his stiff body. She held on. *Come on, Rick. Let me help. Let me share it.*

"All I'm saying is that we got Axle in here. Surely the vet will be able to help him."

Rick patted her back as if he were hugging a great-aunt. "Thanks, Stephanie." He stepped away from her and rubbed his hands down his thighs a few times.

Stephanie tried not to let his dismissal hurt, tried to explain it away as his way of dealing with the anxiety. He was too tough a guy to want to lose it in front of these strangers and his coworkers, but the wall she sensed he had now constructed seemed insurmountable.

He's shutting me out.

The assistant spoke to Rick. "Dr. Bailey will be right out to talk with you as soon as he's finished up in there."

Rick's jaw clenched. "Thanks."

Stephanie wished Rick would look at her, not over her or around her, but actually at her. If she could make eye contact maybe she could read what he needed from her, but he stared ahead, watching the assistant plod away.

As they sat next to each other in silence, Stephanie had too much time to think about Julian Hale. Righteous anger burned inside her, but its companion was a slow vacuum of fear sucking her in. When it came to Julian, she was done asking "what" and "how"; now the most natural next question had to be "who." *Who is next?*

"Mr. Powell?"

Stephanie and Rick rose from their seats. A man looking to be in his fifties wearing a lab coat over his Wranglers stepped toward them. Stephanie noticed his eyes were kind, but behind the kindness she recognized something else that scared her. Pity. Goose bumps ran up her legs and through her heart. *Don't you dare give us any bad news.*

"Mr. Powell, I'm Leo Bailey." He extended

his hand. Rick shook it. "I've finished examining Axle. Why don't we sit—"

Rick cut him off. "I don't want to sit. Tell me how he is." Rick crossed his arms and took on his police stance. "I don't care what it costs. Whatever it takes to make Axle well again, I'll pay for it."

The vet nodded. "Well, Mr. Powell, when I first examined Axle, I was worried we would be having a much more difficult conversation. He's been hurt badly, but you've got a very tough and very determined dog in there."

It was as if Stephanie had sucked in all of their combined worry and then hadn't exhaled for hours. After hearing the vet's hope-filled words, Stephanie's whole body deflated in relief. Axle was going to be okay. She squeezed Rick's hand again, hoping that the good news would thaw the new coldness that had suddenly descended on him, but there was no squeeze back from him. She sensed the frozen wall between them growing taller and thicker by the minute. What had she done? Why was he treating her like this?

Dr. Bailey continued his prognosis. "Thankfully, the bullet missed some vital areas and then exited without too much internal damage. Axle's going to need antibiotics and time to rest and heal, but he'll pull through." The vet flipped through the chart he held. "It looks like Axle has already proved that he is not one to stay down for long."

The vet smiled and dropped the chart to his side. "I have a feeling you haven't seen the end of this dog's heroics yet."

FOURTEEN

How long until he finds us here?

Stephanie sat on the edge of the hotel bed, running her hands along the comforter, picking at the tiny matted balls on the old pilled material. Her eyes roamed her new surroundings, taking in the 1980s pastel decor. A slight antiseptic scent made the room seem uninviting, but at least it was clean and cheap. She was going to owe Rick so much money by the time this week ended. Most importantly, though, the single-level roadside hotel was close to Axle at the vet's office in case he needed them overnight.

Stephanie had always been an introvert, requiring more alone time than other people to recharge, but now she was restless, too keyed up to enjoy the quiet. She needed something to occupy her mind so she could stop wondering if Julian Hale knew exactly where they were.

Rick was next door in the adjoining room with only an interior door separating them. She knew that all she would have to do was cry out for him and he would come crashing in to her rescue. Jason King was in the room on her other side. She stood up and peeked around the curtain into the parking lot. At that moment a sheriff's department patrol car rolled by on the street, and parked in the space directly in front of her room was a truck with Russ Miller in the cab staring at her door. He waved at her. She gave a tiny, embarrassed wave back and dropped the curtain. She was definitely well guarded.

It was too early to sleep, and she had left the book she had started reading behind at the cabin. She paced the room and then stopped to listen. She couldn't hear anything coming from Rick's room. What was he doing? Probably wondering if there was any way he could get out of babysitting her sooner than he had promised Terrell.

Turning on the TV didn't help her restlessness. She flipped through every station, but it all annoyed her. How could the world go on like normal? She felt too jaded to laugh at corny sitcoms and too consumed with her own issues to care about the world's news. She turned it off. What she didn't want to admit was that she was lonely. After spending so much time with Rick and Axle for company, she missed them. She missed Val, too. Maybe Rick would let her use his phone to call her.

Stephanie's hand hovered inches away from the door that separated their adjoining rooms, trying to decide if she should knock or not. He had been acting so distant and aloof, she was sure he wanted to be left alone. But after all the adrenaline and worry over Axle, this letdown was making her feel stir-crazy. She needed to talk to another human being.

She rapped lightly on the door. "Rick? Are you awake?"

The door swung open with so much force, Stephanie popped back.

"What's wrong?" he asked. His brows were pinched together, his eyes searching first her, and then the room behind her.

She put her hands up. "Nothing's wrong."

Why had she bothered him? Her question seemed so stupid now. She stumbled over her words. "I just wondered if I could borrow your phone."

He cocked his head, looking confused. A few seconds ticked by before her words convinced him she truly was okay, and his alert posture relaxed. He turned, leaving the door open behind him.

Returning with his phone, he tossed it to her. "Just keep it with you for now."

She caught the phone down low by her knees, grateful that she didn't drop it. Without saying anything more, he shut the door, leaving her alone again.

"Thanks," she said to the closed door. Then she kicked it, which she regretted when pain shot up from her stubbed toe. She fell backward onto the scratchy bed and dialed Val's cell number. She stared at the ceiling waiting for Val to answer.

"Hello?" The smooth, warm voice of her friend wirelessly crossed the miles and embraced Stephanie's heart.

"Val?" She swallowed, trying to control the flood of emotion.

"Steph? Are you safe?"

Stephanie winced. Her every attempt to talk with someone tonight made them worry something was wrong. "I'm okay."

"Then why do I hear tears?"

"I didn't call to talk about me," Stephanie insisted.

"But how you are is what I care about."

After several moments of silence, Val let out an exasperated sounding sigh. "Oh, all right." She started talking in rapid-fire sentences. "We're all fine. Living in a hotel with kids is about to send me over the edge. The house can be fixed, but it is going to take several months before it is livable again, so we're shopping for a rental. At least we have the swimming pool at the hotel because it is saving my sanity." Val's report ended abruptly. Stephanie heard the deep inhale she took before she declared, "There, you're all caught up on us. Now spill it, *chica*."

Val could be so bossy, but Stephanie loved her for it. She told her friend everything that had happened over the past few days, trying to downgrade the danger they had faced, but Val couldn't be fooled. She kept pressing for more details, peeling back the layers of facts until she got to how Stephanie was feeling about all of it.

"What about Rick?" Val asked. "How's he doing?"

"Rick's..." Stephanie stared at the closed door in the center of her wall. "Rick's fine, I guess. I wouldn't know for sure. He's too busy being a jerk and giving me the cold shoulder."

"I knew it," Val said excitedly. She sounded so happy, as if she had won the lottery or something. "Hee hee. I knew it, I knew it."

Stephanie scooted up against the headboard and hugged a pillow. "Valencia Watkins, what do you *know*?"

"You *like* him."

Stephanie slipped her head under the water line of the bathtub, her curls floating around her. The shampoo fizzed in her ear. *I am not interested in Rick Powell.*

She had denied it on the phone. "It's only been five days, Val. That's too fast to be accusing me of falling for the guy."

"Says who?" Val had said. "Besides, you have known Rick for a lot longer than that. You both needed to be pushed a little to pay attention to each other, that's all."

Stephanie spit air at a bubble on her nose and lathered the hotel's old-fashioned-smelling soap between her hands. *I'm not falling in love with him, am I? Because that could mess everything up.* She could deal with a little crush. Anything deeper than that would be more complicated. Stephanie viciously scrubbed her arms as if she could rub off the doubts along with the dirt.

She had collected so much grime. Lying face-down along the river's rocky bank while a madman used her for target practice could do that to a girl, she supposed. The whole ordeal had left her scraped up and filthy. It felt good to soak it all away.

"I'm not falling for him, Val," she had said.

But Val had only asked her, "Are you trying to convince me or yourself?"

Stephanie had changed her strategy. "How I feel is irrelevant, anyway. Rick is hardly even talking to me anymore."

"Your feelings are not irrelevant. Rick has his guard up. Terrell did the same thing to me when we were dating. It's a sign that you're working your way into his heart. He's afraid of caring about you, especially after watching Axle get shot. It scares him to imagine something like that happening to you. I've got faith in Rick. He'll come around," Val had countered.

"Valencia Watkins, I love Liberia, not Rick Powell. Are you trying to confuse me?"

"And you don't think God has made your heart big enough for both?" Val had challenged her.

Stephanie unplugged the bathtub while Val's question battered around in her head. God had called her to Liberia, hadn't He? She had been so sure that she was supposed to be there, but she couldn't find any open door for her to walk through at the moment. She loved the country and the people too much to believe that God wasn't sending her there. She forced the silly ideas Val had put in her head to slide down the drain with the last bit of dirty bathwater.

As soon as Julian Hale was caught and behind bars, she and Rick would be able to go back to their normal lives and to their own plans for the future. She stepped from the bathtub, determined that Val's teasing would not distract her any further.

She dressed in the same dirty clothes she had worn before the bath, wishing she had some fresh ones. She grabbed Rick's phone and logged on to her email account. Scanning through all the junk mail, her eyes landed on a message from her sister.

Her heart skipped in anticipation. Stephanie skimmed the note, searching for names of the people she missed so much and for word about how Emily's pregnancy was going. Hungry for news, she picked out certain words and phrases, eating them up like an appetizer to take the edge off the hunger before she went back to the beginning and read every word slower. There were stories about Moses and how much he had grown, funny anecdotes about the Liberian people and a few new Liberian phrases Emily had picked up. Stephanie devoured every word her sister had written.

She remembered the threatening printouts from Emily's blog that Julian had sent to her. Julian's hands had reached everywhere. He had messed with every area of her life, threatened everyone she loved. His eyes had seen every move she and Rick had made. How? She stared at Rick's phone, pondering. Then, slowly, she began to see the common denominator. She knew how Julian was finding them.

She was holding it in her hands.

* * *

Rick put his ear to the door to Stephanie's room. Would he be able to hear her if she called for help? After the cold shoulder he'd given her, he doubted he would see her again tonight unless she was in danger. Grandpa Powell would skin him if he saw how he had been treating Stephanie today. He could hear his grandfather's voice saying, "Son, that is not how we raised you to treat a lady."

And Grandpa Powell would be right. Rick knew he was being a jerk, but keeping her at a distance was for the best. All it took was closing his eyes and he could see Stephanie in the cabin last night, her face lit up by the flickering firelight. It took effort not to walk through the door separating them and repeat that closeness. If he didn't keep his distance both physically and emotionally, he would be too tempted and distracted. He had already crossed the professional line and allowed this case to become far too personal. He had to rectify that if he was going to be able to do his job well, and if hurting her feelings a little was the cost of keeping her safe, so be it.

Are you trying to protect her or yourself?

Stephanie's theory had been that Hale wouldn't shoot her from a distance, but she could have been wrong. She could have been shot just as Axle had been. Rick could have lost both of them by that river today. Sure, he had wanted her to learn to defend herself, but he also had treated her shooting lesson more like a date than a true self-defense lesson. And obviously, he hadn't chosen a secure enough location. He had failed to protect her because he was distracted by his attraction to her. He'd been stupid, and he couldn't keep making that same mistake.

His memory replayed the sound the bullets had made as they pinged off the rocks around them. He imagined one of those bullets hitting Stephanie. Rick turned away from her door and paced the room, unwilling to allow his imagination to go any further with that scenario.

Pounding knocks from Stephanie's side of the door startled him. Her knocking was more insistent this time. He yanked the door open.

Stephanie rushed past him and tossed his cell phone away from her and onto his bed as if it were burning her hand. She pointed at it. "Julian knows we're here."

Her hair was soaking wet, leaving dark wet spots on the shoulders of her T-shirt. The protective instinct he felt for her flared. He put his hands on her shoulders and searched her for injury. Her pupils were dilated and her skin pale again, but she didn't look hurt.

"What's wrong?" he demanded.

"He knows we're here."

"How do you know?" Rick went to the window and flicked aside the drapes. The parking lot held the same cars he had seen the last time he had checked, and Russ Miller was still guarding her door. He couldn't find anything out of place. "Did you see Hale?"

Stephanie grabbed his upper arms and turned him away from the window, her grip tight. "Your phone, Rick." She pointed at the bed. "Who's the carrier?"

It was an odd question. "The city has a contract with VoiceOne for all the department's cell phones."

Stephanie covered her face with her hands, talking to him through her closed fingers. "Ahh. I don't know why I didn't think about it when you told me to leave behind all my electronic devices."

"They're the biggest carrier in the nation, Stephanie. Almost everyone I know uses VoiceOne for their cell coverage. What's the connection here?"

She removed her hands so she could look directly at him. "I won a technology grant from VoiceOne for my classroom."

"So?" *Who cares? Is Hale here or not?*

Her shoulders sagged and she collapsed onto

the edge of his bed. "When I won that grant, they sent one of their IT guys to set up my new equipment." She looked up and asked, "Does that ring any bells?"

Rick could feel the snarl on his face as he spit out, "Hale worked for VoiceOne?"

Stephanie nodded. "It's possible to find someone's location through their cell phone, right?"

Rick growled his frustration and started pacing. "Yes. You can ping the cell towers and locate to within three miles of their location, a lot closer if that phone is GPS enabled, which mine is."

How could he have been so stupid? They already knew Hale was a technological genius. Rick remembered the photograph Hale had sent to Stephanie, the one where he put a blanket around her shoulders outside the fire. The image captured a look of tenderness on his own face that had surprised him. Hale must have known that Rick wouldn't stop looking out for her. Matching the police officer he saw protecting Stephanie to the department-issued phone would have been elementary for someone like Hale, especially if he had access to VoiceOne records. Rick reached for the phone to power it down, but Stephanie's slender fingers wrapped around his wrist to stop him. "Wait," she said. He jolted at her touch.

She had the same determined line to her mouth that he had seen on her face outside the Watkins house right before she took off on her own. She had made some kind of decision, and he guessed he wasn't going to like what she had on her mind.

The blue of Stephanie's eyes deepened to navy, the intensity of her gaze imploring him to listen to her. She dropped his wrist, and he immediately missed the warmth of her touch. "We can use this, Rick," she said softly.

"No." Trying to trap Hale wasn't worth the risk it would take to pull it off.

"Yes," she countered. She crossed her arms and lifted her chin in defiance. "You don't get to call all of the shots, Rick. This is my life, my problem."

"We need to power down the cell now and get Hale off our trail. Then we need to get out of here and warn the vet."

She shook her wet head. "No, Rick. What we need is to stop Julian. This phone is our way to do that."

Rick was tired of arguing. He leaned down to reach around her and grab the phone off the bed, but Stephanie blocked him. She placed her hands on his upper arms again, holding him back. Their faces were only inches apart. Rick's chest tightened at the nearness. He swallowed and then stepped back and let her talk.

"We've been in this hotel long enough for Julian to locate us again already. If he suddenly loses our trail he'll know that we've figured out how he's tracking us."

"So what if he knows that we're onto him? He'll have to come up with a new game plan. That will give us time to find a real safe house for once." Rick was ready to take back the upper hand. No more Julian Hale popping up unexpected sounded very appealing. He could take Stephanie far away and leave the work of taking down Hale to his colleagues.

She put her fingertips against her temples and squeezed her eyes shut. "You're not seeing the bigger picture, Rick. Don't you remember what Detective Shelton told us at the hospital? That Julian's pride would be his downfall? This is our chance to trip him up."

She kept her hand on the phone behind her back and out of his reach. "If we play dumb and let him follow us, we can lure him wherever we want him to go."

"I suppose you think I'm going to let you play some kind of bait in order to do that? Because I'm not." Rick widened his stance. He wasn't backing down on that part. He had promised Terrell that he would protect Stephanie as if she were a member of his own family. Terrell would never let her purposefully put herself in danger, and neither would Rick.

"Like you care." She mumbled so low it was almost too quiet for him to hear what she said. Her already-flushed face deepened to a horrified purple. Rick guessed she hadn't meant to say that out loud.

Rick's voice rose a little in volume. "What is that supposed to mean, Stephanie? I don't put my life on hold like this for people I don't care about. I've done nothing but try to protect you."

"And ignore me." Her gaze locked onto a hangnail she picked at on her thumb.

Her words were like a kick in the gut because they were true. He should clear the air right now and let her know it wasn't anything she had done, that he had only been trying to maintain a professional distance, that she shouldn't take it personally. He reached for her. "Stephanie, I…"

But before he could apologize, she popped up off the bed and put her own distance between them. "I shouldn't have said all of that. You're right, you have put your life on hold for me, and I appreciate it so much. I really only want for you to be able to go back to your normal life and not have to be responsible for me anymore." She squeezed her arms around herself. "This favor for Terrell has been too much to ask of anyone."

Tell her you're sorry. Tell her that you've enjoyed being with her and that you care about her safety, too, not just for Terrell's sake. But Rick bit back his apology. It was better this way.

Flustered, Stephanie changed the subject back to Hale. "Aren't you sick of Julian having all the power?"

"Yes, but putting you at risk on purpose is too high a price to pay in order to tip the scales. I'm not going to let it happen."

"Well, it might not be up to you." Stephanie hung her head. "Because I've already called Detective Shelton."

FIFTEEN

Thursday

Rick filled the doorway of Gary Shelton's cubicle. He flexed his fingers, trying to control his anger and annoyance at being called back to Seattle for a chat with the detective. He had to leave Axle all alone in that vet's office hours away in order to humor the man, but he refused to be bullied into using Stephanie as bait. "You do not outrank me, Gary."

Shelton shook his head. "You're right, I don't outrank you, Powell, but those who do are on my side on this one," he said. "And frankly, if your head was in the right place, you'd be on board, too. I'm not asking that much."

Rick's fists clenched tight. It would feel good to knock the smug look off Shelton's face. Gary Shelton was a friend, but not so good a friend that Rick would put Stephanie's life in danger in order to please him.

Am I making too big a deal of this? After all, Shelton was only asking him to stay in Seattle and to leave his cell phone turned on so Hale could track it. Rick wanted to destroy the stupid phone and drive Stephanie far, far away. Maybe that desire was more evidence that he had gotten too close to her and too emotionally invested to do his job well.

But his gut told him that somehow Hale would figure out how to twist this to his own advantage. His intuition also told him that Shelton would see any harm that might come to Stephanie as simply a sad but necessary price to pay for protecting the greater good. Shelton viewed Stephanie as nothing more than a pawn in the big picture.

Rick towered over the smaller man sitting at his desk, but Shelton wasn't backing down. The detective stood to his full height, his eyes turned to steel. "This is our chance to stop this maniac, Rick. It's time to put an end to this cat-and-mouse game you've been playing with him. We can't blow this opportunity just because you are sweet on her."

Rick slammed his fists onto the detective's desk sending papers flying. "Don't try to make this about me. You're the one who has let this get far too personal. You want to catch Hale so badly you can taste it. I'm not going to let you gamble with her life."

"This isn't your call anymore, Rick. It's gotten bigger than you, and if you can't maintain your professionalism, I'll make sure they take you off Stephanie's protection detail."

Neither man paid any attention to Stephanie sitting in her chair inside the cubicle, her face turning a deeper cherry red by the minute. She cleared her throat, drawing the men's attention to where she sat. "I'm sitting right here. Don't I have a say in this?"

The detective answered, "Of course you do" at the same time that Rick growled, "No, you don't."

Her blue eyes connected with Rick's. "Come on, Rick. We've been over this. You know you are tired of playing Julian's game."

Rick glared at her. He *was* tired of Hale's cat-and-mouse game. He wanted Hale to know what it felt like to be the mouse for a change, but he didn't want Stephanie to be the cheese in order for that to happen. If they left the cell phone behind, they could disappear without being followed by Hale for once. That had to be the best course of action to keep Stephanie safe.

She stood up and went toe-to-toe with him. "Well, I'm tired of it. I want my life back."

The detective sat back down in his desk chair;

the smug tip to the edges of his mouth had returned. "Go back and get your dog, Rick. Hole up in another hotel if you want to. It doesn't matter where you two go as long as we make it look like you are still running and trying to hide. In the meantime, we will set up a team to nab Hale whenever he shows up again."

Rick looked into Stephanie's imploring eyes, ignoring the detective. "It's not going to work," he told her. He couldn't care less what Gary Shelton wanted him to do at this moment. This was between him and Stephanie. "Julian Hale is too smart for this. He'll see right through it."

"Then nothing has changed," she said.

Stephanie and Rick breathed in and out in unison. It became a game of who would blink first.

"Fine," Rick said, throwing up his hands. "But we are doing nothing more than keeping the cell turned on. We are not sending Hale a formal invitation to join us, and you are not putting yourself in any unnecessary danger, got it?"

She smiled. "Got it."

Rick kneaded the back of his neck. "You are a real pain, you know that?"

"Yup." She scrunched up her nose. Then she gave him a goofy, crooked smile and held up her index finger. "But I'm cute."

Rick chuckled. "That you are."

The demanding cry of Rick's cell phone ringtone interrupted them, making all three people in the cubicle jump. He unclipped his phone from his belt and stared at it. "Call from," the robotic voice of his phone's operating system announced, "Allison Townsend."

Allie? He blinked at the caller ID on the screen, unbelieving. *Really?* He hadn't heard from her in a year. He had forgotten that he'd added her married name to his contacts. What could she want to talk to him about now all of a sudden?

"Rick, it's Allie." Her voice shook with emotion. "We need to talk. Is there somewhere we could meet?"

He listened to what she had to say. Something had really scared her, but she refused to talk about it over the phone. She insisted they had to meet in person.

"I'll call you back," he told her, and that was as much of a promise Allie was going to get from him now or ever.

After Rick explained Allie's request, Shelton rubbed his hands together.

"Well, look what we have here," he said. "The perfect scenario just dropped into our lap."

Rick could almost see steam coming from Shelton's ears as the gears inside his brain turned.

"You should go meet your fiancée for coffee and take Stephanie along with you. It's a perfect way to draw Julian out of hiding. You ignore Stephanie while you make goo-goo eyes with your long lost love. Stephanie acts all rejected and hurt and wanders off on her own. Meanwhile we watch and hope Hale will try to capitalize on the situation." Shelton looked as though he was enjoying the soap opera scene he was dreaming up, but the idea did not sit right in Rick's stomach.

This smelled of setup. It had to be more of Hale's games. Rick couldn't shake the feeling that they were walking into a trap.

"She is my *ex*-fiancée. And she happens to be married, by the way—let's not forget that important detail."

Gary Shelton wasn't known for his fidelity or for any long-lasting relationships. In his mind that would probably be an insignificant distinction, but Rick wanted Stephanie to know the difference.

Shelton waved off his words as if he were swatting away annoying flies. "Semantics. Just give the woman your full attention and keep your back turned to Stephanie while you're at it."

"It's the 'hopefully Hale will try to capitalize on the situation' that concerns me most," Rick grumbled.

"We'll have more guys than you can count who won't take their eyes off her for a second. You have to trust your team, Rick. Nothing's going to go wrong."

Famous last words, Shelton.

The silver BMW slipped effortlessly between two cars into an open parking spot across the street. *She even parks elegantly.*

The sporty car fit the image Stephanie had created in her mind of the type of women Rick would have dated in the past. Women who were completely unlike her. Allie Townsend's long legs swung out of the door before the beautiful brunette rose from the car and jogged toward the corner coffee shop where Rick and Stephanie stood waiting for her.

Allie swept past Stephanie, leaving a cloud of high-end floral fragrance lingering behind her. Stephanie inhaled the subtle rose and sandalwood tones. It was a lovely scent and a perfect match for the chic woman in front of her. Stephanie tugged at the hem of her dirty T-shirt, remembering she was still wearing the clothes Rick had bought her at the Marysville Walmart several days ago. What must she smell like? She had washed out the clothes in the hotel sink and let them air-dry, but the bar of soap had left them stiff and still dingy. Her other clothes had either blown up in the bomb, or had been left behind at the cabin in their haste to get Axle help. Stephanie shrank back as Allie embraced Rick.

With her immaculate tailored clothing and her flawless makeup, Allie appeared sophisticated and in charge, but her white-knuckle grip on Rick's arms and the way her eyebrows pinched together spoke volumes. *Julian has gotten to her, too.* Stephanie sighed as an almost motherly pity squeezed her heart.

Allie's head snapped to where Stephanie stood. All evidence of fear vanished as Allie's facial features smoothed into a nonchalant expression. A smidgen of curiosity peeked through, but otherwise Allie became a vision of total control. She stepped from the embrace and ran her hands down Rick's arms. "How are you, Rick?"

Sunlight glinted off the giant diamond on Allie's left ring finger, evaporating Stephanie's pity. She wanted to swat the married woman's French-manicured hands away from Rick's arms. *He's not yours to worry about any more,* Mrs. *Townsend.* But she restrained herself, remembering that Rick didn't belong to her any more than he belonged to Allie. With the history the two of them shared, Allie did have more right to Rick than Stephanie, even if she had let him get away. Stephanie remained silent, waiting for Rick to recall that she was standing there, waiting for him to care enough to introduce them.

He didn't.

Detective Shelton had told Rick to "ignore Stephanie while you make goo-goo eyes with your long lost love."

So the charade begins. Stephanie shifted her weight from foot to foot and wondered what she was supposed to do. Detective Shelton hadn't given her very clear directions other than to wander off and feign hurt. That wouldn't take much acting on her part. She had played the third wheel before; why was it bothering her so much today? Rick was playing his part perfectly, however. *Maybe he isn't acting.*

Cars and cyclists passed on the street, braking and honking at jaywalkers. Yuppie-looking pedestrians streamed by their spot on the sidewalk. Stephanie squinted into the bright sunshine, wondering about the people passing her. Which of them were police in disguise sent to protect her and nab Julian, and which were simply real Seattleites and tourists enjoying an unseasonably warm afternoon? More importantly, where was Julian Hale? Could he see her?

A sweet preschooler bumped against Stephanie's leg. The little girl held a red balloon animal and smiled up at her before her mother led her farther down the street. Stephanie watched a college-age boy lock his bike onto the rack next to her. The first real spring weather in many weeks had driven people tired of the drizzle out of doors en masse. The street was full of color and movement and innocent bystanders. What if Julian started shooting at them again in this crowd? Who would get hit in the cross fire?

Allie's gaze moved between Rick and Stephanie. "You two look like you've been through a war zone."

"Something like that," Rick answered her. Stephanie noticed his eyes doing their own scan of their surroundings. He pointed toward the door of the coffee shop. "Can we get inside now?"

Thankfully this gorgeous woman hadn't distracted him too much. Even if he had been giving Stephanie the cold shoulder lately, and was now too wrapped up in this reunion with his former fiancée to remember she was standing next to him, at least he was still the hypervigilant cop Stephanie had come to rely on for her protection.

Allie pouted and flipped her smooth dark hair over her shoulder. "Aren't you going to introduce us first, Rick?"

Before Rick could do the honors, Allie held out her slender hand to Stephanie, keeping her eyes on Rick. "He never was much for manners. I'm Allison Townsend."

Stephanie shook Allie's hand, feeling as though she wanted to fall into a hole. "I'm Stephanie. It's nice to meet you."

"So—" Allie elbowed Rick and winked "—does she know about us?" she asked him, her laugh brittle.

Bile burned Stephanie's throat. Val was right, and Stephanie was the fool. She couldn't deny her feelings for Rick any longer, but this woman from his past was so far out of her league. Stephanie's hand rose to smooth down her frizzy, disobedient hair. This tan, elegant woman with her Coach purse, her sculpted eyebrows and her perfect shampoo-commercial hair was Rick's type, not Stephanie in her frumpy Walmart couture. How had she let this happen? When had she stopped fighting against the attraction? She tried desperately to reel her heart back in, to reclaim it for herself, but it refused to obey.

Allie addressed her next question directly to Stephanie. "Did he mention how he broke my heart?"

SIXTEEN

Rick's blood pounded behind his ears. Allie's accusation left him so enraged, he was speechless. His eyes darted to Stephanie. What was she thinking? If he didn't have to worry about blowing Shelton's little soap opera charade, he would be in Allie's face and have it out with her right there on the sidewalk. *I broke your heart? Are you kidding me?*

His hands shook as he swung open the glass door for the two women to walk into the crowded coffee shop ahead of him. Before he stepped inside, his eyes settled on the shiny new BMW across the street. *Married life appears to be treating her well.*

He had been with Allie when she bought her old blue Honda Civic. It was right after she closed her first big real estate deal. He had never seen her prouder than she was using that commission as a down payment on the car. Apparently a five-year-old Honda was beneath her current social status.

A little bitter, aren't we? Well, why not? Wasn't he due a little bitterness? "I can't do this anymore" were the last words she had spoken to him when he was lying in a hospital bed, followed by zero contact until today's phone call dropped on him out of nowhere. The size of the engagement ring that she had left sitting by his hospital bed had been laughably small compared to the gaudy diamond she was flaunting now.

When she had introduced herself to Stephanie as Allison Townsend, he almost corrected her. She had always been Allie Driscoll to him. Allie Driscoll was the girl in the eighth grade who stole his heart and gave him his first kiss. She was the girl he had thought he wanted to marry. This angular, pretentious woman named Allison Townsend was foreign to him. Her hug out on the sidewalk had felt bony and cold compared to the softness and warmth he had felt holding Stephanie.

Stephanie. There was nothing cold about her. Her smile alone could raise the temperature in a room. It took all his willpower not to look over at her. *Shelton said to ignore her.* Even though he doubted that Hale could see into the coffee shop, Rick still needed to get into character, to play the part of the smitten ex-fiancé. He cleared his mind and let the hissing steam, the baristas' shouts of ready orders and the other patron's chipmunk-like chatter barrage his senses. He had been so tuned in to protecting Stephanie, it was difficult to give in to the noise and chaos and let it distract him.

But when Allie started rattling off her long-winded order for a one-pump, no whip, skinny, tall, vanilla, soy *thingamajig* drink, Rick couldn't help but meet Stephanie's gaze and roll his eyes. She giggled and put her hand over her mouth to stop it. Somehow he expected that Stephanie's order would be much less complicated.

He stepped close to Stephanie and said quietly in her ear, "That girl deserves a raise if she can remember all of that order."

"For sure," Stephanie agreed, her blue eyes dancing with delight.

Drinks in hand, the three of them searched but couldn't find a seat in the standing-room-only shop. Outside, one tiny bistro table with two chairs, not three, remained open. It was too small for the three of them to fit.

One table over from them, a North Face–clad customer sipped his drink as he read a tablet. There was nothing particularly noticeable about the guy—he looked like everyone else out today—but Rick recognized him. He had worked with the guy before. *Nowhere open for all three of us to sit together. Well played, Shelton.*

"I, uh, should, um, let you two catch up." Stephanie stammered.

Warning bells rang in Rick's head. *I don't like this, I don't like this.* Out loud he said, "Are you sure you don't mind?"

Stephanie's face paled. "Not at all."

She pointed down the sidewalk to a clothing boutique. "I'm sure it's been a while since the two of you have talked, and I wanted to check out the store next door, anyway."

Allie plopped down and scooted her chair up to the table. "That's sweet of you, Stephanie." Then she dismissed Stephanie with a blatant head-to-toe perusal of her clothing and said, "Have fun shopping." Rick gritted his teeth. Had Allie always been this snooty?

The empty chair across from Allie would leave his back turned to the direction Stephanie was about to walk. The seating situation would please Shelton, and would maybe tempt Hale out of hiding, but it was mutiny to Rick's training and instincts. As Stephanie moved past him, Rick reached out and stopped her. The bright sun made her eyes a brilliant sapphire, and the hurt feelings he could see in them tempted him to abandon the plan altogether. She had honest eyes that were easy to read. There was never any pretense in Stephanie. He had been such a jerk to her after Axle got hurt. He would need to make it up to her somehow.

"Be careful," he said, and dropped her arm. He willed himself to keep his eyes on Allie instead of turning to watch Stephanie walk away. He had to trust his team to take care of her.

To Allie he said, "Tell me what this is all about."

With his back turned, Rick couldn't see it, but he knew the moment Stephanie was out of earshot because Allie's calm and collected facade melted. She leaned forward and whispered, "Maybe you should tell *me* what's going on, Rick."

"You called me."

"I watch the news. I've seen the coverage of that killer on the loose and heard about that bomb going off at that hotel. I know you're involved. Don't deny it. You can't stay away from that kind of drama."

His chuckle was stiff. "Yeah, that's me, always on the lookout for drama." He drained his coffee cup with one long, exaggerated drink. "So you called to tell me you were worried about me?" He couldn't help the sarcasm.

"Of course I have been worried about you, Rick. Contrary to popular belief, I do not hate you." She sat back in her chair. "But that's not why I called."

Allie dug into her handbag and pulled out an envelope that looked similar to the one that had carried Stephanie's threatening photos from Hale. Rick poured the contents onto the table. Two items fell out: a black-and-white glossy photograph and a small square slip of paper with typed print on it. The photograph was of Rick and Axle walking into the hotel, the place that was supposed to be a "safe" house, on Sunday evening. A crude target had been drawn over top of his image with a red paint marker. The slip of paper had typed notes about Allie:

Allison Townsend (née Driscoll)
Owner of Puget Sound Realty Execs/
SeaHome Property Management
Husband: Attorney, Timothy Townsend
Children: None

Along the bottom, Hale had written the phrase *unresolved heartbreak* in the same chicken-scratch handwriting he'd seen on Stephanie's envelope.

"He called our house, Rick." Allie's year-round tan paled around her mouth as she whispered the words. "It's him, isn't it? It's that killer on the news."

Rick inhaled and exhaled through his nose, trying to get professional control over his rage. "I'm sorry you were dragged into this, Al, I really am."

"That's not the worst of it." Tears pooled, threatening to run her mascara. "He said…" Allie choked down a sob. "He said that I had to tell you he would be willing to make a trade."

"A trade? What kind of trade?"

She quit trying to hold back the flow of tears, and let them streak black down her cheeks. "He said to tell you he didn't mind trading me for Stephanie if you wanted her to live instead." Allie's voice shook again as it had on the phone earlier. "He said to tell you he wasn't picky as long as he gets one of us."

Rick tried to cover one of her hands to comfort her, but she swatted it away. "No. This is what I walked away from, Rick. I told you I wasn't cut out for this." She paused, and then added in a quieter voice, "I'm not brave like you."

"No one is going to die, Allie. Hale isn't getting either one of you. I won't let him."

"Well, he's not getting me. I'm leaving town tonight." She opened a compact and wiped away the mascara mess. She smoothed her hair. When she was composed she said, "Timothy has arranged a trip for us to Cancun." Allie dropped her compact back into her bag and dug out a business card with "Timothy Townsend, Attorney-at-Law" embossed along the top. "Here's Tim's number. Call us when it is safe to come home."

She stood up and slung her purse over her shoulder. She squeezed her arms tight around her waist. "Rick, I know you think I'm selfish…"

"Wanting to be safe isn't selfish, Allie…"

"I never meant to hurt you like I did. But it is what it is." Her brown eyes were full of regret. "And we both know you are better off without me. I only came here to warn you so you could keep her safe, but it looks like you are already doing that."

Rick cleared his throat. "Stephanie and I aren't seeing each other…"

"Well, you should be. She seems like a nice girl. Treat her right, okay?"

He heard the *better than you treated me* part that she really meant. Rick stood and gave Allie a sideways squeeze on her shoulders. "I will. Thank you, Al."

"I mean it. You deserve to be happy."

He watched her leave. He could see her dark hair bouncing as she jogged back to her car.

"Goodbye, Allie." In his mind it was a forever goodbye. *We are done. Go on with your life. I'm free.*

There had been a time when Allie's very presence in a room consumed him. He had loved her. She had broken him, but her power was gone. It was the one good thing in this bleak, stress-filled week, knowing that his heart belonged to himself again. Hale had been so wrong. *Heartbreak resolved.*

Hale had meant to play with Rick's emotions, but instead he had given Rick the gift of closure and clarity. He could see Allie for who she really was now. Comparing her character to the caliber of a woman like Stephanie made him question for the first time whether or not his failure at love had less to do with his career and a lot more to do with the type of woman he had chosen. *Thank you, God, for unanswered prayers.*

His cell phone rang, followed by the monotone voice announcement, "Call from...Gary Shelton."

Rick answered it, spinning in circles as he searched for Stephanie. "Shelton, you had better have good news for me."

Stephanie fingered the hem of a dress hanging on a sale rack outside the boutique. The silk fabric was smooth and the blue color would look good on her, but her mind was far from clothes. Her attention was locked on the cozy-looking couple sitting outside of the coffee shop down the street. *Stop stalking them, Stephanie.*

Her face flushed as she remembered all of the unknown eyes of the cops who were watching her at that very moment. To Rick's coworkers, she must look like a lovesick puppy. She dropped the hem and turned her back on Rick and Allie. *Rick and Allie.* She imagined their picture in their high school yearbook with the "Cutest Couple" caption underneath it.

She stepped around a seagull hopping on the sidewalk and walked uphill to the bookstore next door. She did not like this jealous monologue playing out in her mind. Shouldn't someone dedicated to serving God overseas as a missionary have her mind set on more noble things? She must have something to think about other than the cute boy and his former girlfriend on their little date. She needed to get a grip.

Scanning her surroundings for a possible threat was becoming second nature to her. *Which one of you is watching me?* It was so weird to know she was being monitored, but to still be unable to identify who was doing the watching. Whoever they were, they were good at making themselves invisible.

At first her eyes almost completely missed the man standing a block away on the other side of the street. Other than the bright red ball cap he wore, his drab clothing blended into the crowd. It was his stillness contrasted with the pedestrians streaming past him that finally caught her attention and caused her to squint into the distance to try to see his face.

Warm fear spread to her fingertips, making her feel weightless and outside her own body. He was here. Shelton's plan had worked. She couldn't see well enough to make a positive ID, but every cell in her body screamed that that was Julian Hale watching her.

Her heart hammered, demanding to be released from her chest. She averted her eyes and made herself walk forward. *Play it cool. Make him believe that you don't see him.*

She picked up a book off one of the clearance tables on the sidewalk and pretended to be engrossed in the story of one man's trek across the Sahara on his motorcycle. The words melded into a blurry string as she tried to swallow her panic. She couldn't stand it any longer; she looked up. Where was he now? She couldn't find the red hat. He had moved, but where?

Stephanie slammed the book closed and held it to her chest, clutching it like a life preserver. She searched for Julian, but couldn't find him.

She frantically scanned the crowds, moving farther away from the bookstore.

"Hey lady, you going to buy that book, or what?" yelled the store clerk.

"Oh, no, sorry," she mumbled and tossed the book onto the nearest table. She had to locate Julian. Why had she looked down for so long? She should not have lost track of him. *Look natural. He'll bolt if he thinks you are onto him.*

At that moment, a heavy hand lit on her shoulder from behind her. The touch caused an unhindered scream of terror to burst from Stephanie's mouth. She spun around, fist raised, but instead of Julian Hale, she found a flinching Rick ducking away from her before she swung at him.

He pulled her fists down and wrapped his arms around her. "It's me," he crooned into her ear. "I'm sorry. It was stupid to sneak up on you like that."

Stephanie squirmed to get out of his embrace. "Rick, he's across the street. I just saw him." She frantically spun around and around in circles, searching everywhere for the red ball cap. It was gone. "He was there, I saw him!"

Rick shook his head and grinned. "No, you didn't. You might have thought you saw him, but it wasn't him." Rick's face was shining. "It's over, Stephanie."

She had never seen Rick looking this happy. "How do you know it wasn't him? I saw him. I mean I thought it was him, but I wasn't close enough to see for sure." Rick's calm reaction was confusing her.

He lifted her off the ground and swung her in circles. When he placed her back down and let go, she giggled. "What is that all about? Are you sure you only had coffee to drink?"

"I just have really, really, *really* good news for you."

Stephanie rubbed at the crease between her eyebrows, trying to get her forehead to relax. *Really good news, huh?* So Rick was talking to her again? What had happened to the frozen Rick she had encountered at the vet's office? This guy was so hot and cold. She never knew what to expect from him. It was disorienting to have him change personalities so abruptly.

She urged him on. "And this good news is…"

"Gary Shelton called me." A gigantic grin took over Rick's entire face, making that gorgeous dimple reappear, deeper than she had seen it yet. *That's not fair, God. That dimple is an unfair advantage.*

"And?" Stephanie urged. *Would he just spit the news out already?*

"And, Shelton got a call from the Bellingham Police Department. They pulled over a drunk driver and they got an NCIC hit when they ran him."

She tugged on her earlobe, rolling it between her fingers. *Would you speak English?* "What is NCIC?"

"NCIC stands for the National Crime Information Center. It's a nationwide database for felony warrants. We can run a person's information anywhere in the country and see if they have a felony warrant from somewhere else. When Bellingham ran their driver, they got a hit." Rick paused for another huge grin. "It was Julian Hale, Stephanie. They *arrested* him an hour ago."

She blinked a few times. Her brain was having a hard time processing what Rick was saying. "You mean…"

Then Rick cupped his hand behind her neck, touching his forehead to hers, and said, "You, Stephanie O'Brien, are a free woman."

But she had been so sure it was Julian looking at her from across the street. Her nerves must have been playing tricks on her imagination. She hadn't seen the man's face. He could have been anyone and she would have seen Julian because that's what she had expected to see.

Rick pulled her into a hug. She wrapped her arms around his waist and leaned into his chest. She liked how she tucked easily underneath his chin. She didn't care that they were standing on a sidewalk surrounded by tons of people. And she didn't care that tomorrow Rick would probably go back to acting as if he didn't even know her. Right now, she needed to be held, to feel anchored down, before she could fully grasp the words Rick had told her.

"It's really over?" she whispered.

He pulled her in tighter. She felt his jaw moving on top of her head as he spoke, his voice deeper. "It's really over, Stephanie. Julian Hale is ninety miles away from here behind bars where he belongs. You're safe."

SEVENTEEN

Monday Morning

Stephanie awoke to a kidney shot from a small brown foot. She wasn't sure at what hour Joash and Haddie had transitioned from their sleeping bags in the living room to sleeping with her, but her muscles were sore from being held in unnatural positions for too long.

The foot responsible for her aching kidney belonged to Joash on her left side. He stretched out horizontally, taking up over two-thirds of Stephanie's small full-size bed. Using Stephanie's right arm as her pillow, Haddie sucked her thumb and curled deeper into Stephanie's side.

All of the bed covers had been kicked off them and Stephanie was freezing. She needed to get up and get ready for work, but she didn't want to wake up the sleeping kids this early in the morning. She slid her arm out from under Haddie's head, cushioning the girls' dark curls with her other hand, lowering it slowly, slowly, hoping to escape without waking her. She moved her pillow up against Haddie's side to be her substitute. She scooted down and exited at the foot of the bed. There hadn't been enough room for the three of them to sleep comfortably, but Stephanie was glad the kids had found her, anyway.

Waking up to the two tiny companions had comforted her in such a deep place. She stood at the foot of the bed watching them sleep. Her chest ached with longing. The peace on their faces was beautiful. In his sleep, Joash scooted closer to his sister for warmth. Stephanie spread the covers over both of them.

As much as she loved these two spooning kids, they did not belong to her. Would she ever stand in the dark watching her own babies sleep, or was that the cost of the meaningful life she wanted? She had always said she wanted to be different, to have a life that meant something, and to do something big for God. Maybe giving this up was her cross to bear. She shook her head to free it from the melancholy. She had allowed too much distraction over the past week in the form of Rick Powell. She needed to get her head back on the goal. Especially now that Julian had been arrested, and she was free to go on with her plans. That is if she could figure out what those plans were even suppose to be.

Stephanie rubbed at the kink in her neck as she tiptoed past Val's air mattress on the living room floor on her way to the kitchen. Val had sensed Stephanie's apprehension at being alone and had spent the past two nights with her. Knowing Julian was in jail in Bellingham made her feel safer, but it would take some time before she would be completely comfortable with being alone.

In the kitchen, she started a pot of coffee. Too impatient to wait until it was done, she poured herself a quick cup and then slid the pot back under to finish filling. She wrapped her hands around the steaming mug and gazed outside into the predawn dark.

"Up already?"

Stephanie jumped, spilling hot coffee on her hand. "Val. You're supposed to be sleeping in."

Val shrugged. "Want me to make you breakfast?"

"I'd love it, but there's no time." Stephanie set her mug in the sink and dried off her hand. "I've got to get to school."

Val rubbed her eyes and stretched her arms high above her head. "This early? But it's still dark out there."

"Yeah, but I've been gone all week. I need an

early start." Stephanie dreaded the mess waiting for her after being away from her classroom. It was going to be a long day of retraining her kids in classroom expectations, and catching up on paperwork and planning. The sooner she got to school the smoother her day would be. "I'm going to shower and go. Don't worry about me for breakfast. I'll pick up a bagel on the way."

Val poured herself a mug of coffee. "So have you talked to Rick?"

Stephanie nodded. "He and Detective Shelton are driving to Bellingham this morning. The extradition hearing will be at eight o'clock, and then they can bring Julian back to Seattle."

Val took a long swig from her mug and then turned a teasing grin on Stephanie. "That will be nice, but what I meant was have you and Rick talked about *you and Rick.*"

Stephanie's heart squeezed. She hadn't seen much of Rick at all this weekend. He had come to the early service at church with the Watkinses, but Axle was home from the vet, and Rick had needed to hurry back to take care of him before his work shift started. Stephanie didn't want to admit to Val how disappointed she felt at how little she had seen of Rick or how lonely that lack of contact had made her feel.

"There is no *me and Rick*, Val."

Val blew on the top of her steaming cup and asked, "And why is that?"

Stephanie rolled her eyes. "Okay, matchmaker. I'm not his type. Have you ever met his ex-fiancée? She is so gorgeous. I have never felt like such a hick as I did standing next to her."

"You mean the woman who left him alone when he needed her the most? Allie abandoned him, Stephanie. You are the gorgeous one— inside and out—and Rick sees that, too. I saw the way he looked at you at church yesterday. No matter what you say, I believe that you two belong together. You can't deny that you have feelings for him."

Stephanie closed her eyes and sighed. "Yeah, I do." It was surprisingly freeing to admit it out loud. "But what good do feelings do me? I'm supposed to be a missionary, and isn't that the cost of following my calling? Giving up earthly pleasure, even love if need be, for the greater gain? Look at all the missionaries in history, like Amy Carmichael. She gave up everything to serve God on the mission field."

"Amy Carmichael was obedient to the calling God had on *her* life. You need to be sure of only what He is asking of *you*, Stephanie. And why can't you have both? Serve the Lord and love someone. It doesn't have to be mutually exclusive."

Val was quiet for a moment. Then she continued in a softer tone. "I know this is going to come out all wrong, but I'm going to say it, anyway. Sometimes I wonder if you are afraid of losing God's love, that He'll reject you like your dad did. I don't deny that you love Liberia, or even that God is calling you to serve the people there, but—" she hugged Stephanie around the waist "—you have to live your life, Stephanie. Not your sister's life, not your heroes' lives, only your own life. God's love for you is not dependent on how well you perform for Him. You know that you don't have to earn it, right? That it's a gift."

Stephanie frowned. Her mouth gaped. She opened and closed it several times as she groped for words to explain herself. When she couldn't find them, she shook her head and waved off Val's concern. "Of course I know that, Val. That's not it. You just don't understand. You haven't been there. You haven't seen what I've seen. I *love* Liberia."

"But you want to love Rick, too, don't you?"

Stephanie flinched from the sting of the words. She didn't have time for a heart-to-heart. "I've got to go, Val. Help yourself to whatever you want to make for yourself and the kids for breakfast."

* * *

Rick's knee bobbed. He drummed his fingers on the car's armrest, and then stopped to check the clock app on his phone for what must be the thirtieth time. Shelton was driving as fast as he could get away with, but for Rick, the two-hour drive had felt like five already.

He didn't have to come along. Now that Axle had been discharged, Rick could have chosen to stay at home with him and let someone else go with Shelton to pick up Hale. But Axle was in good hands with Cindy, his retired, dog-loving next-door neighbor, and Rick needed to see Julian Hale wearing handcuffs with his own eyes.

Finally Shelton's phone droned out the last of the GPS's turn-by-turn directions. "Your destination will be on the right," it intoned in its signature science fiction-like voice.

Rick released a breath of relief. *About time.*

Shelton pulled the department's transport van into the jail's sally port and put it into park. "I can't wait for Hale to face the justice he deserves," Shelton said. "I'm going to have a tough time not delivering it myself."

"Me, too," agreed Rick.

The detective reached behind the van's front seat and grabbed his briefcase. "So after this case is wrapped up, are you planning on making a move on the girl, or what?" Shelton asked Rick.

Rick snorted as he climbed out of the van. "Why? Are you interested in her, Gary?" He tapped the hood. "I can always see if Stephanie wants a date with you."

"Watch it, you young punk," Shelton said. Then he winked. "I will say that if I had a better track record with relationships, and I thought for a minute she'd be interested in an old man like me, you might have some competition on your hands."

An image of Stephanie's beautiful face projected on the screen of Rick's imagination, but he pushed the thought away. He might want to pursue it, but he couldn't think about romantic involvement with her. She had plans that didn't involve settling down with a cop. The best he could hope to give her was seeing Julian Hale put away for life, to give her the gift of never having to worry about a killer chasing her again. "Let's just go get our guy and forget about my love life for now, okay?"

"Fine," Shelton said. "But will you take some advice from an old man?"

"Depends on the old man," Rick joked.

"When you find the good one, you don't let her get away." A faraway, wistful expression crossed Shelton's face.

She is "the good one," but I can't ask her to give up her dreams for me. Rick tapped the hood again with his fist. "It's a little late for that. She's leaving for Africa," Rick said. He paused for effect. "She's going to be a missionary."

"A missionary?" Shelton spit out air in disbelief. "With all your good looks and charm, you can't change her mind about that?"

Rick gave him a wary smile. "Not sure that I could or should try to change those kinds of plans even if I was able."

Shelton answered with a small nod. "I suppose we can't get in the way of the Big Man upstairs." He averted his eyes from Rick and shifted his weight. He didn't seem comfortable with the deep turn the conversation had taken. "Whatever you do, though, don't end up an old man and all alone like me, okay, kid? The job isn't worth that kind of price."

A guard opened the jail door and asked, "Detective Shelton?"

"That's me." Shelton shook the man's hand and then introduced Rick. "This is Officer Powell."

The man smiled and offered Rick his hand next. "Adam Kerns. It's nice to meet you both."

Rick shook and returned the grin. "Can't tell you how happy we will be to see Julian Hale in handcuffs. So who do we get to thank for catching our bad guy for us?"

Deputy Kerns smiled. "That would be me. I wanted to be here to meet you guys. I guess I know how that trooper in Oklahoma must have felt when he pulled over Timothy McVeigh. Sometimes we stumble on the bad guys without even looking."

He grinned again. "I'll tell you what, that NCIC hit was quite a shock. Didn't see that coming."

"I'm sure it was." Rick could easily imagine the jolt of adrenaline seeing that warrant pop up on the computer screen would cause.

Kerns scanned the paperwork that Shelton had handed him. "This all looks good. Are you guys ready for him?"

"More than ready," Rick answered.

The deputy spoke into his radio. Rick's fingers were in constant, anxious motion, drumming the air at his side. He heard a buzzer and then the *click* of an automatic lock opening. He strained his neck to peer around the guard to see clearly as another deputy guided a prisoner through the door.

Rick's eyes narrowed as he studied the prisoner. He guessed the man to be in his early fifties, about the same age as Shelton. But instead of the fitness and vigor of the running-addicted detective, this man was slouched over as he shuffled into the room. His face was haggard and unshaven, and under the gray stubble, the man's puffy face and yellow skin tone were those of a heavy drinker. Rick frowned, confused.

Shelton cocked his head as he addressed the guard. "Who's this?"

The new deputy answered him. "This is Julian Hale. Aren't you guys here to pick him up?"

Shelton swore and slapped the clipboard he was holding against his thighs.

Sweat beaded on Rick's neck. *No, no, no, no. Hale couldn't have played us again.* He shook his head and said, "There must be a mistake. This man is most definitely not Julian Hale."

The prisoner's head popped up. The man's whole demeanor changed. He stood straight, color flowed into his cheeks, and his eyes sparkled with hope. "See! I've been telling you that all weekend," the man told the guards. "It's not me they want." He looked back and forth between Shelton and Rick, his eyes wide. "I tried to tell the judge but she wouldn't listen."

"Who are you?" Shelton demanded, his nostrils flaring.

"I *am* Julian Hale. But not the Julian Hale that you want. Maybe there are two of us. All I know is I'm no killer. I'll admit all day long that

I drink too much, and how stupid it was for me to get behind the wheel drunk, but I ain't never killed nobody, never. You've got to believe me."

Shelton shoved the papers back at the deputies. "I appreciate your help," he said. "But we're not taking custody of this man. He's not our guy."

"But we found evidence in his car. His description was dead-on, and his Social Security number fit the NCIC hit," Kerns demanded.

"That's your problem," Shelton told the dumbstruck deputies standing next to the grinning prisoner.

Rick felt sick. Hale must have known about the other man who shared his name, a man with a bad habit for repeatedly drinking too much and then getting behind the wheel afterward. It was like Hale to have a contingency plan set up as decoy. How long had he been planning this? But the deputies had found incriminating evidence in the trunk of the wrong Julian's car. Hale would have had to plant that evidence in the trunk and then watch until the man started driving. After that it would only take a phone call complaining about a dangerous drunk driver on the road, and Hale would be able to play them once again.

Had Hale also hacked into the NCIC database? He would have had to change the Social

Security number and physical description on the warrant. Julian Hale disgusted Rick, but he had to respect his brilliance. When would they stop underestimating this guy?

Rick and Shelton sprinted toward the van. Over his shoulder Shelton called back to them, "We've still got a killer on the loose and more importantly, we've got a woman who's about to become a victim if we don't get to her first."

Winter's fingers clung to the spring morning with damp, bone-chilling mist. Friday's beautiful sunshine had only been a tease. Spring in Seattle would arrive, but not anytime soon. It was running late this year. Stephanie ripped off a vicious bite of her bagel and trudged on through the cold morning. She loved being a teacher. Why was she so blue about going to school? Her heart wasn't in it this morning, but her crankiness probably had more to do with her conversation with Val than it had to do with not wanting to go to work. Stomping her feet to warm up her toes, she continued up the steep sidewalk to the school.

Only a week ago, she had been running from a bomb. She didn't know how to easily return to her mundane life as if none of it had happened. The adrenaline and adventure had made the days seem to fly by, but the closeness she had shared with Rick had made the single week feel ages long, as if Rick and Axle had always been a part of her life. She pulled off another chunk of bagel and shoved it into her mouth. She chewed aggressively, hating how much she missed them. Life had been so much easier when Rick Powell had been nothing more than a cute acquaintance.

Stephanie turned into the nearly empty staff parking lot. Only a few cars dotted the black-top this early in the morning. She slipped off her backpack and dug through its contents in search of her keys. Not watching where she was walking, she collided with a man crossing the parking lot in the opposite direction.

The man helped her regain her footing. Tipping the brim of his ball cap down at her, he said in a hoarse voice, "I'm sorry about that. Didn't see you there."

"That was my fault. I walked right into you," Stephanie chuckled, smoothing her curls. She swung her backpack over her shoulder and looked directly at the stranger.

A pair of dull cornflower-blue eyes peered out from under the red hat brim, taking Stephanie's breath away. She stumbled back a step. "But…but you're…"

He grabbed her elbow and shoved the tip of a gun into the fleshy part of her stomach. Ice filled her veins. "Hello, Stephanie. Surprised to see me?"

He shoved her head into his chest. There was no one in the parking lot to hear her muffled screams.

EIGHTEEN

Bumping around in the backseat, Stephanie forced herself to recall everything she had ever heard or read about self-protection. It was all bits and pieces, nothing concrete. The one thing she did remember was that whatever it took— biting, screaming, kicking, scratching— it was crucial that a victim never allow herself to be taken into an attacker's car.

That was great in theory, but there hadn't been time to fight back before Julian's gun was thrust into her abdomen. Her mind had been busy turning over her conversation with Val, and because she thought Julian was in jail, Stephanie's guard had been lowered. Before her fight instinct could think about kicking in, Julian had already held a cloth over her face until everything went black. She woke up in the backseat of this car, her hands and feet bound in zip ties and a blindfold tied tightly around her eyes.

Stephanie wiggled in the seat, trying to find

a comfortable position. She tasted blood in her mouth from gnawing on her inside cheek so hard. *I've got to get out of here.* Dread weighed heavy on her mind, making it difficult to strategize. Stephanie worked to toss off the feeling of doom. If she was going to survive this, she had to stay positive. Although she could feel the vibrations of the moving car, she couldn't see behind the blackness of the blindfold to determine what direction they were traveling, and she couldn't get a feel for how much time had passed. How long had she been passed out? The driver was so silent, she wasn't even completely sure that it was still Julian behind the wheel.

Faces of everyone she loved loomed in her mind. She could see them in such vivid detail, these people she had to see again, people who made her want to live, but of all the faces, it was Rick's that stood out the most. *I want a chance to know him, to love him.* Why was that clear to her now, when she couldn't act on it? It was too late.

She wondered what Julian planned to do with her. Stephanie curled into a fetal position. She wasn't afraid of being dead. She had hope. It was the process of dying, and the pain Julian Hale had in store for her, that terrified her the most.

* * *

The hours it took to drive back to Seattle from Bellingham had been pure torture for both men. They tried to reach her, but after it was clear Stephanie wasn't answering their calls, Rick and Detective Shelton had taken turns yelling at people through their cell phones. Eventually there was nothing left to do but rely on their friends in Seattle to find Stephanie until they could get there to help. They had settled into a mutual stony silence while Shelton obliterated every speeding law along I-5.

Finally, Shelton had dropped Rick off at the department and the two separated to start the search in their own way. Rick met Terrell at Stephanie's house.

"Anything?" he asked Terrell as he burst through her door. Terrell shook his head. A lump rose in Rick's throat at the look of sadness in his friend's eyes. Rick nodded. "Okay, I'll start looking in the back."

Standing in the doorway of Stephanie's bedroom, Rick choked on a sob, forcing himself to swallow his grief. Her bedroom reminded him of her—feminine and cozy, but clutter-free. A chilly breeze tossed gauzy blue curtains around her open window. He pulled the curtains aside to see that the window had been left open a crack. Had Hale ever been inside her house?

Rick knew he had spied on her through the webcam, but he wondered if Hale had ever come inside her home. Nausea rolled at the thought.

They were all fools. And he blamed himself the most. Until he had seen Hale behind bars with his own eyes, he should never have let Stephanie out of his sight. Hale had lulled them all into a false sense of security, and Rick had fallen for it right along with the rest of them. After all of the technology tricks that Hale had pulled off this week, why hadn't any of them thought that he might still be manipulating them? They had ignored the precedent, and Stephanie had disappeared because of their complacency.

Hale probably hadn't snatched Stephanie from her house. Val and the kids were the last to see her after she said goodbye to them and left for work, and they had still been here when the school called looking for her. It was more likely that he had picked her up somewhere along her walking route to the school. A girl at a bakery Stephanie had stopped at remembered selling her a bagel, but that was where her trail ended.

Rick leaned against the door frame. Maybe being here was nothing more than his need to feel close to her, but they had no clues yet to work from. They needed to start somewhere, and her room was as good a place to start as any. He stepped across the threshold feeling as if he were entering a sanctuary.

At her desk, Rick riffled through her papers and books, doubting he would find anything helpful, but doing a thorough job of it, anyway. He would never forgive himself if he missed something important. He spotted a scrapbook in the hutch above the desk. He pulled it down and sat down on her bed. Stephanie had hand-lettered the word *Liberia* across the entire page and then filled in the letters with bright colors and textures. He didn't know she was so artistic. He mourned for all of the things he didn't know about her yet. Was she even still alive?

He flipped through the pages, his eyes hungry to find her face. In every picture, the poverty of both the country and the people photographed was evident, but that wasn't what Rick noticed. Instead, he noticed the beauty and the joy, especially present in the photos that had Stephanie in them. In his favorite picture she smiled wide, dressed in a brightly patterned dress. Her hair was wrapped up in a head scarf, and she leaned against an African woman wearing a matching outfit. The two women were so different yet there was an evident sisterhood between them. Their huge smiles spoke of a love he knew nothing about, a love he wanted to know.

Stephanie! Where are you? How do I find you?

He gasped for air, his own powerlessness suffocating him. It was becoming an all-too-familiar emotion. The first time had been the night he was stabbed and left for dead. His own mortality and lack of control over his life had been so clear as he bled onto the pavement. He had felt the same way on Wednesday listening to Axle's pain-filled howls by the river, hating how helpless he was to make it better for the dog he loved. And each time Julian Hale had been successful at threatening Stephanie's safety without being caught, Rick had been humbled. He might wear a gun and a badge, but he wasn't in charge. He couldn't control life no matter how much he might want to, and he had absolutely no idea how to save Stephanie now.

He closed the book and tossed it aside onto her bed. Sliding off the bed, he hit his knees. *Lord, help.*

"Home sweet home." Julian's voice chimed from the front seat. So it was still Julian with her. She heard the engine turn off.

Stephanie stiffened. This might be her only chance left to slip out of the zip ties and make a run for it. She wiggled and writhed, trying anything to loosen their grip, but nothing worked.

The back passenger door opened next to

her head, and she felt the cool air on her face. "Where are you taking me?"

"Now what fun would it be if I told you everything? Let's see if you can guess." Amusement edged Julian's voice as he taunted her.

"I'm tired of your games," she told him.

"Well, that's too bad, because the games are only beginning. I'm not done having fun yet," he said.

His arms slipped under her armpits, yanking hard. Her eyes and arms were useless but she blindly whipped her bound legs around like a mermaid tail, trying to make it as difficult as possible to drag her. He had gotten her into a car, but now that she was outside it, she was fighting back with everything that she could throw at him.

Stephanie screamed, "Help me! Someone help…"

But Julian was prepared. Intense bursts of electricity coursed through her body, paralyzing her. She couldn't move or speak; she could only feel the pulsing pain.

"You like that?" Julian asked her, the energy level increasing in his voice that had been lacking only moments ago. "That was fifty-thousand volts of electricity. You took it pretty well, Stephanie. I'm impressed."

She wished for her eyesight so she could anticipate the next shock and prepare herself for the pain that could come again on his next whim. Behind the blindfold she wouldn't have any warning.

"What was that?" she asked him.

"That, my dear, was a Taser. I'm sure your boyfriend has one on his gun belt."

Stephanie flung her head in the direction of Julian's voice, tightening her body to prepare for more pain. "I'm going to leave these barbs attached to you. That means I can fire again anytime I need to. Now," Julian asked her, "would you like another round of electricity or are you done fighting me?"

"I'm done," she whimpered.

Julian dragged her tied-up body indoors, her legs bumping over gravel and grass and finally up concrete steps. She heard a door slam behind them before he dumped her onto a soft couch. She strained to hear anything. She inhaled deep breaths through her nose, searching for any scent that might clue her in to where Julian had taken her. Nothing struck her as familiar.

"I'm going to remove the blindfold now, and you will remain calm or I will shock you again, is that understood?"

The agony from the jolts still fresh, Stephanie nodded her agreement. Julian Hale would not take her out without a fight, but for now she didn't mind avoiding further pain in order to get her sight back. If she could see, she would have all of her senses to help her plan.

She felt Julian's fleshy fingers cold against her skin as he unwound the fabric. The blackness receded, but the pressure from the tight blindfold had blurred her vision, making it difficult to get her bearings even with it off. Lights were on, but she sensed it was still daylight, afternoon maybe? She twisted her head around looking for visual cues to where Julian had taken her.

"Where are we?" she asked him.

"You don't recognize where we are? Interesting…" He stretched the word out as if her ignorance genuinely fascinated him. Her vision was still a little blurry, but from the couch he had tossed her on, she could see a flat-screen TV and a bookshelf. The room was masculine and boring, some kind of bachelor pad. *This place needs a woman's touch.*

Julian sat on the ottoman in front of her. His thin ash-blond hair fell in straight bangs that looked like he used a ruler to cut them. She could see his bald scalp through his wide, precise part. Pale hair, washed-out eyes, pallid skin, and monochromatic clothing—Julian Hale's appearance was as lifeless as his eyes.

"Are you going to tell me where we are?" she asked him again.

"I answered that question outside. If I tell you where we are, what fun would that be?" Julian stood and slapped his thighs. "Well, why don't you settle in and search for some clues while you wait? I need to have a little chat with your boyfriend."

"He's not my boyfriend," she yelled at his retreating back.

Terrell tapped on the wall of Stephanie's bedroom. "Hate to interrupt a brother in prayer, but we've got something."

Rick scrambled to his feet. "What did you find?"

"I didn't *find* anything, but Julian Hale just called the department claiming responsibility for Stephanie's disappearance."

Rick froze. "Did he say where he's holding her?" If they knew where she was, they might be able to rescue her. Hope swirled in his stomach and chest, wanting him to grab hold.

"No. He didn't mention location." Terrell ran a hand across his hair. *Now what?* "How much experience do you have with hostage negotiation, Rick?"

"None," Rick answered. "Why?"

Terrell scratched his head. "Better learn quick, because Hale made it clear. He speaks with no one but you."

NINETEEN

Terrell Watkins and Gary Shelton listened in on another line while Rick grabbed the blinking phone in front of him. "This is Powell."

"Hello, Rick."

Rick's lips stretched into a snarl at the sound of Julian Hale's arrogant voice. Of all the things Rick wanted to say, a pleasant greeting didn't appear anywhere on that list.

"Hale," he finally choked out. He wanted to reach through the phone line and strangle the man, but he had to stay calm and keep Hale talking.

"I assume that you have already searched Stephanie's house, as well as mine again." Hale said. "Find anything interesting?"

He's controlling the conversation.

Rick needed to flip this around, to tip the power back in his direction. He couldn't allow Hale to continue pulling the puppet strings.

"Let's skip the small talk and get to your demands," Rick told him.

"You need a little practice in negotiation, Officer Powell. Aren't you supposed to be building trust, assuring me you have my best interests at heart?"

Rick huffed. "You and I have too much history between us to be anything but honest. We've exchanged bullets, Julian. I think we can skip the pretense of liking each other and move past the chitchat. What do you want?"

Hale chuckled. "This is true," he agreed. "So, I've been waiting patiently. Have you figured out our location yet?"

He's having fun with this. It is all a big game to him. Rick hated to answer that he didn't know where Hale and Stephanie were located. The SWAT team was pre-alerted, waiting to hear where to show up. They had been told, "We've got something going down but we don't know where to send you yet. Hang tight." Nothing in Stephanie's house had pointed them to her location, and all of their attempts to locate her cell phone had failed because her phone was powered down.

Using enhanced caller ID, dispatch advised that Hale's call had come in on a prepaid phone without GPS. They were working on figuring out which cell tower he was using.

Rick directed the conversation down a different path, hoping Hale would slip in a clue. "Is Stephanie okay?"

"Are you changing the subject? So, that would be a no, then, you don't know where we are?" Hale snickered. "I'm disappointed. I thought I made it so easy to find us. Maybe if I stay on the line a bit longer, you'll trace the call like they do in the movies."

The yellow pencil Rick had been twirling snapped in two.

Hale's taunting continued. "Or maybe you'll be smart enough to find me on your own. I'll call back in fifteen minutes and see if you've made any progress."

Rick waited for Hale to hang up, but he started to speak again. "Oh, and Rick."

"Yes."

"You better hurry. Stephanie's time is running out."

Stephanie had heard Julian's threats to Rick. *How much time do I have left?* Her body began to shake, first in her legs, and then the trembling moved up her spine and then back down to her bound hands. She tried to control the shaking with deep breathing, but she was having a hard time calming the fear.

"Julian?" she whispered. "Why?"

He lunged at her, his pale skin blotchy and his empty eyes bulging. Stephanie flinched from his hot breath so close to her face. Sneering, Julian spoke to her between gritted teeth. "Don't talk unless spoken to first."

Anger sparked in his eyes, revealing a sign of life underneath his unnaturally placid exterior. His reaction startled her. It was so unlike Julian to be so passionate about anything. What was it about her question that had aroused his temper? Maybe he didn't like her using his name.

"I need to understand why this is happening." Her arms ached from being pinned behind her for so long. "Why me?" she squeaked out.

His face contorted, his fight against an internal storm playing out on his face. She winced. Would he shock her again?

"Why *not* you, Stephanie? I kill people. That's what I do. Are you so special you think someone else deserved to die in your place? Who should it be instead? Allison Townsend, perhaps?"

"Wasn't I kind to you?" Stephanie asked him. "What did I do to you that made you hate me?"

Julian's face relaxed back into its familiar void-of-emotion expression. "You annoyed me when you slipped away like you did, but if it is any comfort to you, Stephanie, I do not hate you." He turned his back to her and walked to the bookshelf. He picked up a framed photograph from a shelf. "In fact, in my own way, I highly value you," he said.

Value me? Enough to take my life away from me?

"You should consider yourself fortunate. The pain I inflict before you die will allow you to feel, to know for certain that you are alive." He turned his dead eyes back on to her. She recoiled from the sickness she saw in them.

Julian returned his gaze to the photo he held in his hands. He lowered his voice even further. "You won't believe me when I tell you this, but I will be doing you a favor."

She choked out a half chuckle, half sob. "I should thank you for killing me?"

"Yes. You should. You won't have leprosy of the soul like me."

Leprosy of the soul? What was that supposed to mean? Blood pounded between her ears, making her head ache. Julian's mind was too twisted for her to follow his train of thought.

He remained silent for several heartbeats. His voice was only a notch above a whisper when he added, "You will die in pain, but you will die loving and being loved."

Her eyes stung and blurred. She shivered. The desperation of this man chilled her. Her heart lurched with pity at the thought of his emptiness. *He's jealous of me?* Of all the things to envy her for, Julian had chosen her ability to give and receive love. *Me, the abandoned and fatherless, the single woman with no relationship.* He had picked the one thing she thought she lacked the most.

The slideshow of faces started to march across her mind again. She saw Terrell and Val and remembered how lost and lonely she had been when she wandered into the junior high youth group they were leading. They had taken her under their wings back then, and all these years later they were still loving her. She saw the faces of Joash and Haddie, and those of the countless people she knew in Liberia. She felt again Axle's warmth when he guarded her in the hotel stairwell from the bomb. She felt again Rick's arms around her. All the people she loved and who loved her back. It had never occurred to her before this moment just how rich in love her life was, but a stranger had been able to see it and want it for himself.

"You are loved, too, Julian," she whispered.

"What do you mean?" His body snapped into a rigid, defensive stance. His eyes narrowed. Currents of hatred sparked off him like the electricity he had shot at her. Stephanie pulled back into the couch as far as she could. "Do you mean by your *God,* Stephanie? Are you trying to *save* me?"

Warmth started in her core and radiated through her. It was unexplainable. She sat facing a killer who planned to torture and kill her; she should be terrified, yet strangely she was basking in peace. Cleansing tears flowed unhindered down her cheeks. Julian had given her a gift, the chance to see the truth even if he wouldn't accept it for himself. A Bible verse Terrell had made her memorize all those years ago in youth group floated to the surface. "The LORD appeared to us in the past, saying: 'I have loved you with an everlasting love; I have drawn you with unfailing kindness.'" She was loved. And so was Julian.

"Yes, Julian. You are loved by God. If you want it, it's yours."

Julian slammed the photo back on the shelf. "You can keep your little missionary spiel to yourself." He laughed a manic cackle. "You don't need to practice your speeches. You won't be running off to Africa anymore. What are you going to do now that you can't earn those brownie points?"

Julian's words seared her heart. They were basically the same sentiment that Val had tried to tell her that morning. She had believed the lie that if she worked hard enough, did something grand enough, then maybe, just maybe, God wouldn't reject her as her father had done.

"God's love is a gift," she stammered. "I couldn't earn it even if I tried." Light filled her mind as more truth dawned. "And nothing will separate me from that love. Even if you kill me, Julian, I'll still have it."

Julian cocked an eyebrow. "Well, you will have a chance to test that theory soon enough."

Courage and peace she could not explain continued to buoy her, but her curiosity had one more question needing answered. "Why are you waiting, Julian? Why haven't you killed me already?"

His chuckle was low and soft this time. "Your time is coming soon enough, but I have big plans of my own, and I need you to stay alive long enough to bring me my audience. We wouldn't want your *boyfriend* to miss out on all the fun, would we?" He waved her off, dismissing their conversation. "If you'll excuse me, I need to make a phone call."

As he stepped away from the bookshelf, Stephanie looked at the photograph he had re-shelved. She saw a typical department store backdrop behind a smiling couple. The picture could have been taken at any mall and could be of anybody's grandparents. But these particular smiles, this particular couple, Stephanie recognized.

She sat straighter. It made perfect sense.

Of course he would come here. It was a case of good old-fashioned revenge. She glanced again at the framed photograph of Rick's smiling grandparents. A larger version of the same photograph hung on their cabin wall.

The police had invaded his home. Now Julian had invaded one of theirs.

Stephanie surveyed her surroundings with a new appreciation. She was sitting inside Rick's house.

Rick tapped his fingers on Shelton's desk, waiting for Hale's next call. Other officers were out searching for Stephanie while he sat on his rear end. He wanted to be out there with them, doing something more productive than sitting here waiting for Julian's next chess move.

Shelton pointed at him. "Back on line one."

Rick punched the button and lifted the receiver. "Julian. What have you got for me?"

"Ha! What have I got for you?" Hale laughed at him. "I gave you homework. I'm getting bored sitting here waiting for you to come over and play. Trust me, you don't want me bored."

"We know where you are," Rick lied.

Shelton ripped off a sheet of paper from a notebook and slid it in front of Rick. *Call is coming from somewhere in or near Greenwood. Finally a clue.* Rick grinned at the detective and then at Terrell. Julian hadn't taken Stephanie outside of the Seattle metro area, and he was hiding in an area of town they all knew well. Both Rick's and the Watkinses' houses were in Greenwood. Together they should be able to come up with ideas of where to search. It was just a matter of time. But how much time did they have?

"What happened to all of our history keeping us honest, Rick? If you knew where I was, you'd be here by now." Hale cackled again, but there was another sound Rick strained to hear behind the laugh.

At first he wondered if he was hearing things, but he heard it again. It was definitely Stephanie's voice screaming in the background. He jumped from his chair. "Rick, we're in your house. Rick! We are…inside…your house. I saw a picture of your nana and…"

The next sounds made his stomach drop. He closed his eyes as the easily recognizable *zzit, zzit, zzit, zzit, zzit, zzit, zzit,* sound of a Taser firing blended with Stephanie's screams of pain.

"Hale, stop!" Rick bellowed into the phone.

Shelton and Watkins had scrambled away already, alerting SWAT and sending cars.

"Well, I guess I won't be bored for long," Hale said. "But you need to understand something, Rick. I am in control here, not you, and not the hordes of police you've probably already sent this way. You better stop them if you want her to stay alive."

Silent beats followed, and Rick wondered how he should respond. But Hale wasn't finished talking. "If you think you're man enough to take me, come on over, but you better come alone."

TWENTY

At the command post, Rick swung open the door of the mobile home that served as the SWAT team's Tactical Operations Center and stepped inside. All of this planning and talking was taking up precious time. Hale knew they were onto him. How much longer would he allow Stephanie to live? Rick's heart screamed *hurry up and get her out of there,* but his brain and training knew proper planning was critical to success. Despite how much he wanted them to, the SWAT team couldn't storm the house without cause. Unless the threat to Stephanie's life was imminent, they'd keep trying to negotiate. Rick took a deep breath to calm his panic and shook hands with the SWAT commander.

The commander swept a hand toward TV monitors. "We've got cameras up on the windows of your house. Tell me what we're seeing here."

The image was partially blocked by the

wooden slats of his window blinds, but Rick recognized the room and the people in it. Hale stood with his back to the window, gesturing wildly as he made some kind of speech. Tears pricked behind Rick's eyes when he spotted Stephanie lying bound on the floor. He held his breath until he saw her foot move. She was still alive for now.

Rick handed the commander the sketch he had made of his home's floor plan and pointed out the location of the room they were viewing. "That's my den. You enter the living room from the front door. The den is here, behind that wall."

The commander nodded, studying Rick's drawing. "Be prepared to take your position soon. Since you are without your K-9, we'll make you point man on the front entry team." He patted Rick's shoulder with a heavy hand. "Don't worry. We'll have your friend out of there soon."

Rick stood next to Terrell, waiting for the order to take their positions. It felt strange to be working without Axle, but Rick was glad the dog had been with his neighbor getting the rest he needed to recuperate instead of at home when Hale showed up with Stephanie.

An officer walked past them and into the

hostage negotiation trailer. Rick rubbed his hand across his mouth. Were they going about this the right way? The scurrying activity of the command post reminded Rick of Hale's demand that he come alone. They were a few blocks away and hidden from Hale's view for now, but soon the team would move and prepare to strike. What would Hale do to Stephanie when he discovered there was a small army camped outside?

Rick wiped the sweat off his forehead. How much longer would they have to wait? He gazed around his neighborhood, seeing the familiar landscape in a new light. He was so close to Stephanie, yet so far away.

Only slightly over a week had passed since he and Terrell had prepared just like this to serve Hale's warrant. He couldn't have known that morning how much would change in only a week's time, especially not how much his own heart would change.

He reached into his pocket and felt his fingers wrap around the coin he always kept there. Grandpa Powell had given it to him at his swearing-in ceremony for SPD. Rick didn't need to take it out of his pocket to know what was engraved on the coin. He had carried it for over seven years; the words were written on his memory. First Corinthians 16:13: "Be on your guard; stand firm in the faith; be men of courage; be strong."

Be men of courage. What if Stephanie did survive? Would he pursue a relationship with her?

He turned to Terrell. "Sarge, I..."

Terrell interrupted him. "We're going to win tonight, Powell. I can feel it. Don't lose hope."

Be on your guard. Rick looked up to the sky. "I shouldn't have left her alone. How could I have not seen that we were falling for another one of Hale's tricks? I should have driven up to Bellingham right away and confirmed Hale was in that jail cell with my own eyes." Guilt ate away at Rick's gut.

Be strong. "I don't know how you can do it."

"Do what?" Terrell asked him.

"You know..." Rick struggled for the words he wanted. *"Love."*

Instead of laughing at him as he expected, Terrell turned his wise eyes toward Rick with a look of compassion. "Love requires us to do the opposite of what we are trained to do. That's why it is so hard for cops to do it. We have to disarm and allow ourselves to be vulnerable."

"How did you do it?" Rick swallowed. "With Val, I mean." He shouldn't be bringing all of this up now, but he needed these answers. If Stephanie survived, he would have a choice to make.

"It wasn't easy, but I couldn't live without her. Val was worth the risk," Terrell said. "And I didn't want fear to rule my life."

"What about your kids? Don't you fear for their safety?"

Terrell looked away and nodded, thinking. "Outside of what God allows, there is no guarantee of safety in this life. I could be an accountant instead, and it wouldn't change a thing. Our lives are in His hands and we are safest inside His will. My kids' dad is a cop and that isn't a surprise to God. He can handle it. He's got them." Terrell paused. "He's got Stephanie, too, Rick."

Stand firm in the faith. Rick hung his head. "I want that kind of faith."

"Then ask for it." Terrell placed a hand on Rick's shoulder. "Look. You and I—we know the darker side of life. We have to face it every single day and don't have the luxury of pretending it isn't there. We put on our badge and our gun and we try our best to fulfill our calling to serve and protect, but at the end of the day when we strip it all off, we know we are still only men underneath. We fool ourselves if we don't. That's why the real battle has to be done on our knees. That's how I do it."

Rick's cell vibrated, letting him know a text was coming through. When he saw it was from his neighbor, Cindy, he scanned it quickly. He groaned. "Oh, no."

"What?" Terrell asked him.

"It's Axle. My neighbor took him with her when they evacuated. He freaked when they got to her friend's house and bolted. They've been looking for him, but can't find him. She thinks he might be heading this way."

Rick could just imagine how agitated the dog must have been during the evacuation process. But he couldn't go looking for him now. *Please watch out for him, Lord, until I can go find him. Thank You.* He was still so out of practice, the praying felt rusty. But he felt the loosening of his own grip as he took his first baby step toward more faith.

"He'll be okay. We'll find him after this," Terrell assured him.

One of the SWAT guys interrupted. "It's go time, gentlemen."

During the last electric shock, Stephanie had fallen off the couch to the floor. Julian had pulled the trigger three times after her attempt to alert Rick to their location. As he prepared to fire a fourth shot, she begged him, "Please. Not again."

She didn't regret trying to pass the information on to Rick, but she wasn't sure if she had even succeeded. Had he heard her? She was paying a painful price for her act of rebellion. If he did hear her, was he coming?

"Every time I pull the trigger it lasts for five seconds. Feels like longer, doesn't it?" Julian turned the weapon around in his hand, admiring it. "This was a good purchase. I like it."

He squatted down next to her and put it to her temple. She wanted to be tough, but she couldn't help but whimper at the thought of another round of shock. He grinned, apparently pleased at her reaction. "You and your big mouth ruined my agenda. Officer Powell wasn't supposed to show up for another few hours, after I finished with you."

Julian stood up. He put the stun gun down on an end table and pulled a pistol from his waistband. He turned it over, admiring it. "Guess I'll just have to be flexible and go with plan B." He squatted back down so she could see him. He placed the gun in her line of sight. "I'll give you a break for now. Think of it as a little intermission before the final act."

He waved the gun around a bit. "What's your weapon of choice, Stephanie? Gun or…" He walked back beside the couch and placed a large bundle on the floor where she could see it.

Stephanie cringed. More dynamite?

"Which do you prefer? Quick gunshot wound?

That's not usually *my* preferred method, a bit too quick and cliché for my taste." He pointed to the dynamite. "Or do you and Rick go out together in a romantic blaze of glory?"

Stephanie rested her forehead against the carpet and prayed. She understood Julian's goals better now. She had been wondering why he was waiting to kill her, why he was giving the police time to get there. He was luring Rick here so he could kill them both. They had defied him and ruined his plans. Now they would pay together. She wished there were some way to warn Rick about the dynamite.

Bullet or bomb? She couldn't make that choice. Silence was her only response.

Stephanie was afraid, but as she prayed, her breathing slowed, the peace from earlier continuing to bathe her. Tears flowed silently as she lifted up all the people she loved in prayer. She prayed for her sister Emily's baby, the niece or nephew she would now never know. She prayed for Joash and Haddie and the future ahead of them. She prayed for Val and Terrell, and finally she prayed for Rick.

Lord, I want to live. I want Rick to live.

Julian's face perked up in attention. He must have heard something he didn't like. He moved away from her toward the window. She couldn't see him, but she could sense his agitation and pacing. He was back on his cell phone.

"I see your men out there. I gave Officer Powell the chance to be a hero. It wouldn't have ended like this if he had just done what I told him to do and came alone. You tell him her death is on him, because this ends now."

Stephanie jumped at the sound of Hale's cell phone crashing against the wall.

Julian walked back into her line of sight and pointed the pistol at her face. "It looks as if your boyfriend made the choice for you."

Stephanie screwed her eyes shut tight and started praying one last desperate cry for help. Her prayers ceased at the sound of shattering glass. Deafening explosions and blinding white light brought dust and chunks of plaster raining down from the ceiling. She had always wondered what dying would feel like. It sounded as though she was about to find out.

Rick lined up in his position with the front entry team, his heart pounding in his ears. He remembered Terrell's words: *The real battle has to be done on our knees. That's how I do it.* If that was Terrell's secret, then Rick would follow his lead. *Lord, make me firm in faith, stronger and braver than I am on my own. If You allow Stephanie to live, I promise I will let You teach me how to love her right, no matter what it costs me. I'll trust You.* It was all he had time to think before the "Go, go, go, go" screamed into his ear.

It was a beautifully executed dynamic entry. The windows of his house shattered as the 40 mm wood batons blasted the windows, followed by the mesmerizing strobes of flashbang grenades detonating inside. One swing of the battering ram demolished his front door and they were inside. Rick sprinted, the first of the front entry team to penetrate the house. They had mere seconds to reach Hale before he recovered from the shock and disorientation and shot Stephanie.

Find her, find her, find her chanted through his mind, propelling him forward. One way or the other, it would all be over in a matter of minutes. Soon he would know if he would get the chance to tell Stephanie that he loved her. He searched through the chaos around him. He coughed out dust. *Be alive, be alive.*

Rick struggled to recognize the place as his own through the haze. He rounded the corner to the living room and saw Stephanie's body, bound and lying motionless on the floor. He ran toward her, but movement in his peripheral vision made him turn.

The tip of Hale's gun shook from the tremor

in his unsteady hands, but it was pointed right at Rick's head.

Rick spun and fired, *pop, pop, pop, pop.* Hale dropped his gun, swaying like a tree about to topple. Rick knew he had fatally wounded Hale, but he couldn't let down his guard until he was sure it was over. Instead of dropping as Rick expected him to do, Hale raised and flicked to life a lighter. He staggered toward a large bundle on the floor.

Coldness spiraled through Rick's belly. *It's dynamite!* "No! Don't do it!" Time stretched as Rick lunged toward the man.

A deep, throaty snarl came from behind Rick and before he could reach Hale, a blur of brown fur shot past him. A dog leaped into the air; his jaws opened wide and latched onto Hale's arm, preventing him from detonating the dynamite.

Unable to fight the effects of the gunshot wounds any longer, the light in Julian Hale's eyes dimmed and then extinguished. His body fell over dead. The lighter rolled from his lifeless hand.

"Axle! *Aus!*" Rick commanded Axle to let go of Hale. He squatted down and rubbed Axle's head. "Where did you come from, buddy?" Rick had never been more proud of his dog than he was in that moment. "*So ist brav! So ist brav!*" Rick praised Axle over and over again in German. "Good job! Good job! You saved us, buddy!"

Stephanie rolled over, disoriented. She felt the vibration of boots stomping about her, but she was deaf from the explosion. It was like a silent nightmare. She had watched Julian's body swaying above her, his gun raised. She had squeezed her eyes shut tighter with each muffled gunshot that followed.

When she opened her eyes, she had been shocked to see Axle hanging from Julian's arm. Julian had swayed only once more before he toppled over and landed on top of her, his body limp, lifeless.

Boots stopped in front of her, and Axle licked her face. She could hear the distant echo of the word *clear* repeated over and over again. Then the weight of Julian's body was lifted off her and she could see Rick looming above her. He slit the zip ties, setting her arms and legs free. Stephanie grabbed his offered hand and he jerked her to her feet, shoving her forward, prompting her to run for the door.

It had happened so fast, leaving no time to clear her mind. The only objective was to escape before any dynamite detonated. She stumbled out into the coolness and sucked in air. She had prepared herself for death, but now she was very much alive. She tried not to fall as they rushed down the steps.

Rick swept her up into his arms and carried her far from the house. He dropped to his knees beside a tree, but he didn't let go of her. His strong arms held her to him. Burying his face in her hair, they rocked together, not speaking. His body heat warmed her, driving away the shock. She was aware of nothing around her, not the SWAT team and bomb squad members running in and out of the house, not the flashing red-and-blue lights. There was only Rick. Rick was all she saw, all she felt. She was alive and she was in his arms. Slowly, her hearing improved, and she could hear his voice.

"I've got you. You're safe. I'm never letting you go."

Stephanie wrapped her arms around his neck. Looking up into his shining eyes, she knew she was rescued. She kissed his stubble-covered chin. He tipped her face up, and his warm, soft lips covered hers.

TWENTY-ONE

Friday
Two Weeks Later

Stephanie walked down the hallway toward her classroom carrying a stack of photocopies for the day ahead. Her principal leaned out the door of his office and called to her. "Hang on, Stephanie. Before you go, I need to talk to you for minute."

"Sure, Jim. What's up?"

She followed him into his cramped office. Photographs of the Pop Warner football team he coached lined the walls. Fifteen years' worth of elementary-aged football players grinned back at her. It was strange to think that many of those boys in the older photographs must be men by now, with kids of their own. On the edge of his desk sat a photograph of Jim's oldest daughter's wedding from the previous summer. It was a cozy, messy space, but it was still the principal's office, and Stephanie couldn't help but feel like a kid in trouble.

"Everything okay?" she asked Jim as she sat down in the hard plastic chair that he pointed her to.

"Just fine," he assured her. He picked at a hangnail without making eye contact. "I know you've had a rough few weeks. You've had a lot on your mind. Normally I wouldn't want to bother you with this right now, but I've put this off as long as I possibly can." He sat down on the edge of his desk and folded his arms. "I need to have all of my staffing decisions set for the next school year."

Stephanie wiggled in her seat. *Here it comes*.

"I need to know for sure what you plan to do next year." He finally looked her in the eye. "I put a contract in your mailbox. If you're staying, I need it signed by the end of the school day."

The blonde woman behind the desk handed Rick his credit card. "You can have that back now," she said.

He slipped the card into his billfold and returned it all to his back pocket.

She typed with the tips of her fake red nails. Then she grabbed paper from the printer and folded it into two envelopes and handed them to him. "I believe that is all you need for now.

When we confirm the final details and itinerary, I'll have more for you."

"Thanks." Rick stood and offered his hand. "I appreciate all of your help. I know this isn't something you deal with on a regular basis. You were able to get an amazing deal for these."

She shook his hand and grinned. "No, thank *you*. This was all new for me. I definitely don't get requests for that destination too often. It was quite the learning experience. But most importantly…" She winked. "It's so romantic."

Rick tapped his open palm with the envelopes and returned her grin. "That's the goal."

Stephanie slid the bookmark between the pages and closed the book. It was a cliffhanger, and now her students would have to wait all weekend to find out what was going to happen next in their story. It might be cruel, but "Leave them wanting more" was her guiding philosophy when it came to their read-aloud times. She had an innate sense for where to stop reading, knowing how to pull them in, hook them and then leave them dangling over the cliff. She waited for the begging to begin.

A collective groan engulfed her. "No. Not yet, don't stop."

There were many times in the past when she had let her students talk her into reading more.

She was sure they would try it again today. The kids reveled in the victory of convincing her to abandon whatever was next on her agenda. When it came to books, she was a total pushover—anything for the sake of a great story. "I really shouldn't..." she would often say, and then they would know they had her. The kids always ate it up, and so did Stephanie.

Their school pulled its enrollment from neighborhoods where it would be tough to round up very many books at all. Yet here they were, all thirty kids completely engrossed, begging her to keep reading to them. Moments like these thrilled her and whispered to her heart, *See, your life has purpose here, too.* She glanced at her desk where the unsigned contract sat, knowing she had to decide soon.

Stephanie leaned against the back of her high stool and pulled the Newberry Award–winning book into her chest. If she wasn't so excited about what was coming next, she might be tempted to keep reading until the bell rang to go home for the weekend.

"We'll pick up here on Monday." She gave them her wickedest grin. "You'll have to wonder all weekend long what is going to happen next." More groans pelted her.

"Just one more chapter. Please," begged a boy named Jaxon.

"Sorry, Jaxon, we have to stop. We have a special guest speaker coming today, remember?"

Right on time, the door opened, and Axle trotted in, his head alert and his chest puffed up with pride. His wounds were healing nicely and he looked healthy and happy. Behind Axle, holding the leash was Rick. The sight of him sent a rush of blood to Stephanie's cheeks. She blinked. *Hello, guest speaker.* She blinked a few more times. *Stop staring, Stephanie. Your students are watching.* It was going to take time for her to get used to the idea that this gorgeous man in uniform loved her. She cleared her throat and said, "Class, these are my friends Officer Powell and his K-9 partner, Axle."

A girl named Kylie raised her hand but didn't wait to be called on before she blurted out, "Is that your boyfriend, Miss O'Brien?" Nervous giggles tittered around the classroom. Stephanie chose to ignore the question, but Rick leaned in and whispered into her ear.

"Yeah, Miss O'Brien. Am I your *boyfriend*?"

If her face was red before, it was on fire now. She led the way to the front of the classroom. Leave it to kids to be direct.

"Get out the questions you've written for Officer Powell and show me what your best attention looks like." Stephanie stood a little taller as her kids made her look good. They scrambled to follow her directions. It took only seconds before all of their desks were cleared of everything but a single sheet of paper, all their arms were folded, and thirty pairs of eyes were staring at Rick expectantly.

Rick leaned toward Stephanie's ear and whispered behind his hand, "Wow. Impressive crowd control. Sure you don't want to become a cop?"

Never in a million, trillion years. She leaned toward him and whispered back behind her own hand, "It's all in the training, Officer Powell." She shrugged and then, before turning back to the class, she winked and added, "I might be able to give you a few pointers."

Rick rewarded her flirting with a flash of his dangerous dimple. If she wasn't careful, she would forget she was standing in front of her classroom and get lost in banter with Rick. She addressed her students. "Remember class, best manners." Stephanie pointed her first two fingers at her own eyes and then turned the fingers toward the kids. "I'll be watching from the back."

The kids laughed, but held their attentive postures. A warm sense of satisfaction filled her. They were good kids, and she cared about them so deeply. Stephanie threw out her hand toward the students, "Okay, Officer Powell, they are all yours."

She sat down at the round table in the back of the room to watch. "Miss O'Brien told me to tell you some stories about my dog, Axle," Rick told the class. He stroked Axle's fur and then cocked his head, squinting his eyes as if he weren't convinced that was such a good idea. "She said you would want to hear all the good stories about how Axle is a hero, but I'm not sure if I should. I wouldn't want to scare you or anything."

The kids leaned farther forward. Stephanie giggled. *He's good. Definitely knows how to hook a room full of ten-year-olds.* She felt her own body leaning forward, captivated by Rick's charisma in the spotlight. Who was she fooling? He knew how to hook the teacher, too. Everything about Rick captivated her. This was nothing new.

The bell rang, announcing the end of another week. Her students slammed shut the journals they were writing in and shoved them into desks or backpacks, scrambling to be the first in line to go for the weekend.

Stephanie stationed herself in the doorway as she did at the close of every day. "High five, handshake or hug?" she asked each exiting student. Kylie chose a high five. Jaxon surprised her by requesting his first hug of the school year. Miguel stuck out his hand for a quick, shy shake. Down the line she said goodbye to each student for the weekend.

After the last hug, she turned back into the empty classroom. She grabbed her lesson plan book and sat down in one of her students' desks. Each day she chose a different desk to sit in before she left, praying for the student who sat in it. Today she chose Jaxon's desk. His dad was up for parole soon, and she prayed that when he came home it would be good for Jaxon. The boy had come so far this school year and was blossoming before her eyes. *Thank You, Lord, that I've been able to watch the work You are doing in his life.*

Stephanie opened her planner and traced her finger over the photograph of Moses. She really did need to ask Emily for a more current picture of him, but this was Moses as she remembered him in her heart, the age he had been the last time she held him.

She stared ahead at the whiteboard with all her notes written on it in dry-erase marker. She liked seeing the classroom from the students' point of view. It gave her perspective.

Today had felt normal for the first time since she had come back. She had wondered how long it would take for her to readjust to everyday living without the constant threat of death hanging over her head. It had happened sooner than she expected. It had been a sweet day. Rick and Axle's visit being the sweetest part.

Slipped between the pages of her planner was next year's contract. She pulled it out, fingering the paper until the edges started to curl. Stephanie clicked her pen open. The pen hovered over the paper, shaking. She squeezed her eyes tight. She knew what she needed to do. All of the doors to Liberia were closed.

For now.

With a settled heart, she opened her eyes and signed her name, making her decision firm. Liberia owned a part of her heart—it always would—but sitting here in Jaxon's desk, she knew that this school held her heart, too. Someday she would go back and serve the people of Liberia, but when she did, she would be motivated by love and gratitude, not because she was afraid of losing God's approval. She put down the pen, content. Joining Him in the work He was doing right here in the lives and hearts of her students, that was a meaningful life, too.

Rick stood outside Lincoln Elementary, leaning against his patrol car. He could see into the ground-floor windows of Stephanie's classroom.

She was sitting in one of the students' desks, working. He pulled out his phone and texted her. Look out your window. Can you join me?

He felt his own phone vibrate as her answer came through.

On my way out. :)

Rick grinned as Stephanie left the building and walked toward him. Her steps were light, almost skipping. Watching her made him feel weightless. As she drew near, he saw that her smile reached her eyes. She was happy, and that made him happy. He wanted to spend a lifetime making her feel that way. He hoped the envelopes in his pocket would be his first step in accomplishing that.

"I should finish planning for the week…" she told him, glancing over her shoulder at the school.

"No, you shouldn't. You should go get some coffee with me. Besides, I brought you a present." He reached through the open window of his car and pulled out a sticker. It was a silver Seattle PD badge he kept to pass out to kids. "I think you've earned this, partner."

He peeled off the sticker's backing and stuck the badge to her shirt. "There, it's official."

Stephanie giggled. "Does that make me Deputy O'Brien?"

He mocked a heart attack. "Deputy? You're killing me. Unless you are planning on working for King County, let's try Officer O'Brien."

Her face turned red. "Oops. Guess I've got a lot to learn."

"Training starts now," he told her, pulling her into his arms.

Rick took both of Stephanie's hands in his, then he cocked his head and gave her the signature squint she found so adorable. "So, have you given any more thought about what you are going to do next year?"

His question made her realize how happy she was to have the decision made. She nodded. "Actually, Jim called me into his office this morning and gave me until the end of the school day to make my final decision."

Rick's grip tightened on her hands. "And?"

"I signed the contract," she told him. "I finished signing right before I got your text, in fact."

He exhaled, and a slow smile spread across his face. "And you are okay with that decision?"

Axle rubbed against her legs. She leaned down and petted the top of his head, returning Rick's smile. "Rick, I'm better than okay with that."

"Good." He seemed giddy with excitement. "Because I have another present…" He held two envelopes out to her.

Confused, she opened them and pulled out travel documents, plane tickets and an itinerary. Shocked, she looked up at Rick's grinning face. Chills ran up her body. Gratitude and love washed over her as she realized what she was holding. "Are these…?"

He nodded. "Tickets to Liberia for this summer. Tickets for two."

Stephanie grasped the papers to her heart. It felt as if her chest couldn't hold all of the joy. She choked on her emotion, unable to speak.

"I've already put in for the time off." Rick said. "And I've made arrangements with your sister."

He pulled her back into his arms; it was uncomfortable pressing against his bulletproof vest and gun belt, but it was right where she wanted to be. "I love you, Stephanie. Liberia is a part of who you are, and I want to learn to love what you love. I know you wanted to go back there full-time. This is only a short-term trip for now, but it's a start."

She lifted her tear-soaked face and found

his lips, hoping her kiss would say what her voice couldn't.

He pulled away. "Coffee?"

"Yes, please."

"How about every morning for the rest of our lives?" he asked her. It felt as if he was asking for much more.

Stephanie nodded, speechless.

His laugh was music. "Are you sure you are ready to be involved with a cop? You know better than anyone what that could mean, and the price you might have to pay because of my job."

She repeated his words back to him. "I love you, Rick. Being a cop is part of who you are. It's important and noble work. Let's do this—" she waved the tickets, and then tapped her police badge sticker "—all of it, together."

He clasped her hands in his. "You're sure?"

"I'm beyond sure. Are you sure?"

"I know what I want out of life, and you are what I want. But I was afraid I might be moving too fast for you."

She shook her head. "Not after all that we've gone through together. We've been on the relationship fast track. I know that you are what I want, too."

His grin was huge. "Well, in that case, Axle, give the lady her other present."

"There's more?" She wasn't sure her heart could hold any more.

Axle trotted back to her side and sat at attention. She hadn't noticed before that there was a small box attached to his collar. Her hands trembled as she detached it.

Rick put his fingers over hers before she opened it. "Not yet. Hold on." He hollered over her shoulder. "I think it's safe for you all to come out of hiding now."

Out of nowhere, the entire Watkins family appeared at her side. Haddie snuggled up to Stephanie and wrapped her sweet little girl arms around Stephanie's waist. Terrell put his arm around Joash while Val attempted to take video on her cell phone. Val was shaking and crying so much, Stephanie doubted the video quality would be worth watching. None of that mattered to her, though. All she cared about was being surrounded by these people, to bask in her rich life of love.

Rick lowered to one knee and said, "Stephanie O'Brien, will you do me the honor of becoming my wife?"

All she could do was nod. Finally she squeaked out a tearful, "Yes!"

The Watkins family erupted in cheers and whoops and hugs while Axle barked joyfully and ran in circles.

Rick stood up and pulled Stephanie to him. Their bodies melted together in a kiss of promise. She forgot about the world around her. She didn't care about the catcalls from her friends. She and Rick were lost in each other and their dreams for the future.

Joy enveloped Stephanie. She hadn't been looking for Rick Powell, but God had brought him, anyway, as a gift to her. He had given her more than she could have asked for or imagined.

She had had her plans, but God's were better. Rick lifted her off the ground, taking her breath away as he squeezed.

Much better.

* * * * *

Dear Reader,

Thank you for joining me on Rick and Stephanie's adventure. These characters stole my heart. Their story is fictional, but there were many autobiographical elements that made them feel real to me.

I can easily relate to how both Rick and Stephanie were affected by fear. I hope you celebrated with them as they became more aware of God's amazing grace and love. He is so worthy of our trust.

The country of Liberia owns a piece of Stephanie's heart and mine. This book was written before the recent Ebola outbreak in Western Africa. I hope you will join me in praying for the people suffering from this horrible disease.

Thank you for reading *Targeted*. I am excited about connecting with readers. You can find me on Twitter (@BeckyAvella), or my author Facebook page. I also contribute to Team Love on the Run (teamloveontherun.com), a fun blog and online community for fans of inspirational romantic suspense who want to extend their reading experience. If you don't have online access you can reach me c/o Love Inspired Books, 233 Broadway, Suite 1001, New York, NY 10279.

Becky Avella

LARGER-PRINT BOOKS!

GET 2 FREE
LARGER-PRINT NOVELS
PLUS 2 FREE
MYSTERY GIFTS

Love Inspired

Larger-print novels are now available...

LILPDIR13R

REQUEST YOUR FREE BOOKS!
2 FREE WHOLESOME ROMANCE NOVELS
IN LARGER PRINT
PLUS 2
FREE
MYSTERY GIFTS

HEARTWARMING™

Wholesome, tender romances

HWDIR13R

ReaderService.com

Manage your account online!
- Review your order history
- Manage your payments
- Update your address

> ### We've designed
> ### the Harlequin® Reader Service
> ### website just for you.

Enjoy all the features!
- Reader excerpts from any series
- Respond to mailings and special monthly offers
- Discover new series available to you
- Browse the Bonus Bucks catalog
- Share your feedback

Visit us at:
ReaderService.com

RS13